QUARTERBACK
WALK-ON

QUARTERBACK WALK-ON

BY THOMAS J. DYGARD

William Morrow and Company

New York   1982

Printed in the United States of America.
1 2 3 4 5 6 7 8 9 10

Library of Congress Cataloging in Publication Data

Dygard, Thomas J.
  Quarterback walk-on.

  Summary: When the fourth-string quarterback for
a Texas college team suddenly finds himself next
Saturday's starter, he has a plan for winning.
  [1. Football—Fiction] I. Title.
PZ7.D9893Qu [Fic] 81-18715
ISBN 0-688-01065-2 AACR2

For Elizabeth McNamara Dygard, with love.

1

The craziest week in Denny Westbrook's life began, actually, at two o'clock on a Sunday morning.

At the time, Denny was sound asleep in his room in Burwood Hall, the campus home of all the members of the Sutton State Cowboys football team. There was nothing happening in the athletic dormitory to awaken Denny or any of the other players from their deep sleep.

Barely ten hours had passed since the Cowboys had wrapped up a 24-14 victory over the Gordon Tech Engineers. The victory extended the Cowboys' unbeaten record to six in a row. They were riding at the top of the standings of the Southwestern Big Seven Conference. The championship seemed within their grasp. They were virtually certain to receive an invitation to one of the major postseason bowl games. They stood fifth in the national rankings of both the AP and UPI and might move up a notch with this latest victory. The four teams that ranked higher than the Cowboys had won also. But the Gordon Tech Engineers were a national football power, like the Sutton State Cowboys. The decisive triumph was bound to increase the Cowboys' stock with the voters in the national polls.

Denny, of course, had not played in the game. Denny never played in the Cowboys' games. At five feet, seven inches tall, weighing one hundred and forty-five pounds, Denny Westbrook hardly had the physical stature of a big-time college football player. He lacked, too, the speed and natural ability that enabled some smaller players to make up for their shortcomings in size and strength.

Denny had not even made the long trip with the team from Texas to Tennessee to play Gordon Tech. Denny was not on the Cowboys' traveling team. Only those who might be called upon to play rode the team's charter flight to road games. Nobody, including Denny, expected him to see game action. He had watched the game on television in the sitting room at Burwood Hall.

But Denny was on the Sutton State Cowboys football team. He dressed out for the home games. He donned the pads, jersey, cleated shoes—the full uniform—and watched the games from a place on the sideline. In a way, the effort was just a lot of wasted motion. Denny knew that the Sutton State Cowboy coaches were not ever going to wave Denny Westbrook onto the field at quarterback. But the Cowboys required every member of the squad to dress out for home games, and Denny always did, standing with his helmet in his hand watching the action on the field.

Denny Westbrook was a walk-on—a student not recruited, invited or encouraged to attend Sutton State, much less invited to come out for the football team. He showed up on campus unannounced, registered himself for classes, signed himself up for the football team, was issued a practice uniform, was assigned a locker, and began attending the practice sessions. That had been four years ago, when he appeared at Sutton State and enrolled as a freshman.

Some walk-ons turned out to be all-Americans. They were the high-school players, late bloomers in either ability or growth, who were completely over-looked in the frantic scramble for talent by the coaches of the major football schools. They walked onto the field in anonymity and played their way to stardom. But not Denny. He had known from the start that it would never be that way for him.

Sutton State, with its tradition as a winner in big-time college football, attracted outstanding athletes from all over the country to its campus in the sandy, barren flatness of West Texas. These players were the giants and the speedsters, the strong-armed passers, the shifty runners, the sure tacklers, the powerful blockers—the makings of championship football.

Among them, on that first day four years ago, Denny Westbrook was an object of amazement. The

11

other players blinked in disbelief. The crowd milling around the basement of the field house on sign-up day was composed of large, muscular young men—except for one.

Denny, wearing a T-shirt and jeans, seemed even smaller than he was.

"Hey, Flea!" Scott Morrison called out good-naturedly. Scott Morrison, like Denny, was a freshman on that day, but he had already earned the well-deserved nickname: Earthquake Morrison. He had the bull neck, the brawny shoulders, the huge biceps of the dedicated weightlifter. "I hope your insurance is all paid up."

Denny smiled back at the roars of laughter. But Denny Westbrook never let a wisecrack go unanswered. "I hope yours is, too," he said. "When you trip over me, you've got a mighty long fall to the ground." Everybody hooted at Earthquake Morrison.

Tim Van Buren, with the lanky build and the strong hands that clearly labeled him a pass receiver, grinned and said, "I've always heard that dynamite comes in small packages, but after all. . . ."

Denny had heard that line most of his life. He smiled back at the laughter again. "Dynamite just blows up once, you know," Denny said, "and then it's all over."

"Shucks," Tim said. "And I thought we could nickname you Dynamite."

"Right, you can't," Denny said, and they didn't.

12

Denny never harbored any illusions about playing quarterback for the Sutton State Cowboys. In high school, he had been an adequate quarterback—but nothing more. Sheer perseverance won him a place on the team. He was small. He did not have the strong arm necessary for bullet passes. He was not a particularly elusive runner. He lacked the superb physical coordination that every top athlete brings naturally to the game. So at the end of his senior season in high school, none of the college coaches wrote to Denny, as they did to some of his teammates, expressing interest. Certainly none of the college coaches came calling on Denny, pleading the case for their school. None called on alumni in his hometown to apply pressure. Denny Westbrook, adequate as the quarterback of his high-school team, was not college football material. He certainly was not material for the likes of the Sutton State Cowboys.

But Denny selected Sutton State as his school for only one reason: football. Since he had been in the sixth grade, Denny Westbrook had known that he wanted to be a football coach.

Sure, having a record of playing greatness behind him would be helpful. Sure, a famous name as a player was a great asset to a young coach starting out. But for Denny, that was not to be, and Denny realized this truth early. He knew by the ninth grade that he would have to become a coach without ever having been a great player. He would have to make up in knowledge, shrewdness, and cleverness what he lacked in brawn, speed, and coordination.

Denny figured that the best place to learn football was with the best coaches and with the best players. That simple bit of logic brought him to the tumbleweeds and the sandy flatness of West Texas, to Sutton State.

Under Wally Polk, their coach for twenty years, the Sutton State Cowboys had become perennial powers on the college football scene. They had won the championship of the Southwestern Big Seven Conference eight times in the last ten years. They always were ranked in the top ten teams of the country by the AP and the UPI. They had played in postseason bowl games in each of the last fourteen years. At Sutton State, football was important, and winning was the tradition. The Cowboys had built their record and achieved their goals with a mix of outstanding players and the coaching brilliance of Wally Polk, acknowledged as one of the game's most brilliant innovators. Sutton State was a good place to learn football, Denny figured.

Before his freshman season was half finished, Denny Westbrook had found his niche in the football team. He still filled that niche as he headed toward the end of his senior season. He was the quarterback of the redshirts. Every college team has what it calls the redshirts—players fated not to see action in a varsity game. Some are relegated to the redshirts because of

14

low grades. Scholastically ineligible to compete in intercollegiate athletics, they put in a year with the redshirts while trying to improve their grades for the next season. Some of the redshirts are transfer students, sitting out the required year of residency before they become eligible to play for the varsity. Others are players saving one of the four years of their eligibility for a season when their chances are better, after graduation takes its toll of the varsity lineup. And some of the redshirts, like Denny Westbrook, are there because they are too small or too slow or too unskilled to win a place on the varsity team.

For Denny, the role of the redshirts' quarterback seemed perfectly suited to his needs. Each week, on the practice field, the redshirts ran the plays of next Saturday's opponent against the Cowboys' first-string defense. As the weeks rolled by, Denny directed the redshirts' offense in the I-formation, the wishbone formation, and various combinations of spread formations. He learned them all. He had to learn them in order to run them against the Cowboys' defense. He became familiar with the strengths and weaknesses of each of the formations. He also saw the defenses the Cowboys were setting up to throw against the different styles of play. He learned what worked and what didn't work, and why. The education was what Denny Westbrook had come to Sutton State to get.

The fact that he did his playing during the week in a scrubby uniform before the indifferent stares of a few practice-field fans and then rested on Saturday while the fans cheered the varsity never bothered Denny.

On the weekend of the Gordon Tech game, Denny was one of the cheering crowd of students who turned out to greet the bus from the airport when the team returned shortly before midnight.

"Great game," he told Tim Van Buren. The senior split end had caught two passes for touchdowns. One of them was a diving stab that the television crew reran three times, unable to believe that Tim really had made the catch.

An impromptu pep rally erupted at curbside in front of Burwood Hall, where the players were streaming off the bus. The roars hit a deafening pitch when Wally Polk, the grand old man of Sutton State football, emerged. His gray hair was thinning, and he was a little stooped, but he still showed the Cowboys the way to victory. He smiled and waved his right arm loosely at the crowd. He walked in front of the bus and got into a car with his wife for the ride home.

Wally Polk had told Denny once, "If you were six inches taller, fifty pounds heavier, and could pass and run, you would be the best quarterback in America today."

That was one wisecrack Denny had let pass. He knew that coaches did not have to be tall or heavy. They did not need to pass or run.

Tim Van Buren and Denny watched Polk's car disappear into the night. "Louie was really having a hot day," Tim said. Louie St. Pierre was the Cowboys' quarterback. He was a sure all-American. With his quick release and deadly accuracy, he was one of the best passers in the country. "Louie was really hot," Tim repeated.

Denny smiled. "With you on the receiving end, I could be hot," he said.

"Maybe you'll get into the game on Saturday," Tim said.

Denny glanced up at the tall receiver. The question of Denny Westbrook taking the field in a game was coming in for more and more discussion as his collegiate career wound down toward the finish. The players were pulling for him, especially the seniors. After four years of watching him direct the redshirts—taking the shots from bigger players, always hopping back up, never complaining—they had come to like and admire Denny.

"Fat chance," Denny said. The answer was his standard one. And this time, as always, he managed a smile when he spoke.

"It's Allerton."

"Uh-huh," Denny said. The Allerton Lions had lost two games. They were nobody's pushover. But this year they were not of the caliber to be a tough test for the Cowboys. The victory should be easy for Sutton State. Denny knew what Tim was implying: If Sutton State runs up a big lead, why not give Denny Westbrook his chance? For Tim and several of the other players, the move to get Denny Westbrook into a game had become a crusade of sorts.

"This may be the week," Tim said.

Denny had no illusions. "No way," he said.

But that was before the craziest week in Denny Westbrook's life got started.

2

Bad news comes in threes, as they say, and the next two days proved the truth of the saying for the Sutton State Cowboys.

The first news came early Sunday morning and, at the time, did not strike Denny as either disastrous or even surprising.

Denny was up early as always on a Sunday during football season. He dressed quickly and, without shaving, headed for the field house to view the game film from the day before with the coaches. Denny was not required to view the game films. He didn't need to see them. He had not played in the game. None of the errors on the playing field were his. He was not going to play in next week's game either. There were no corrections in his play necessary to assure the Cowboys of victory on the coming Saturday. But Denny, alone among all the players, always attended the screening. He listened carefully to the comments of Wally Polk and the assistant coaches. He took notes in a loose-leaf binder and, upon returning to Bur-

19

wood Hall, organized the notes into what was becoming Denny Westbrook's personal textbook of successful football.

Coming down the stairs and turning into the corridor in the basement of the field house, Denny noticed that the door to Wally Polk's office was closed. The coach and his assistants—some or all of them—were holed up inside. Denny could hear the voices. The words were indistinguishable. The closed-door meeting was odd, especially in the wake of the big victory over Gordon Tech. But Denny thought no more about it.

He walked down the corridor to the screening room and turned in. The student manager, Ernie Watson, was threading the game film into a projector.

Ernie turned. "Did you see the bulletin board?" he asked.

"No, why?"

Ernie's expression changed to the knowing look of the inveterate gossip. He was obviously pleased to be able to deliver the news first. "Take a look," he said. "Just take a look." He turned back to threading the film.

Denny, puzzled, walked back into the corridor. He glanced at Wally Polk's office door, still closed with the vague mumbling of voices coming through it.

Denny walked down the corridor, scanning the large expanse of bulletin board. It was littered with clippings from newspapers, telegrams and letters from

20

well-wishing fans, practice schedules, trip arrangements for road games. Denny saw nothing unusual in the array of items thumbtacked to the corkboard.

"Back this way," Ernie said. He was leaning out the door of the screening room. He glanced quickly in the direction of Wally Polk's office to make sure the coaches still were ensconced in their closed-door meeting. He pointed to a spot on the bulletin board. "There," he said. He ducked back into the screening room.

Denny walked to the point indicated by Ernie. He squinted at the writing on a piece of Wally Polk's letterhead, fixed to the bulletin board with a thumbtack at each corner. The message was typewritten. At the top was the single word: *Notice.* Below was the message: "Louie St. Pierre has been suspended for one week for infractions of training rules." Nothing more.

Denny shoved his hands in his trouser pockets and stared at the note. He was not surprised. Louie St. Pierre had been asking for it. He made a joke of all the Cowboys' rules. Denny could count more than a dozen instances, this year and last, when Louie had returned to the dormitory well beyond the hour of curfew. In more than one case, Louie smelled of liquor when he came sneaking in, and once he spent a night in the bathroom at the end of the hall, violently ill. Louie always got away with it. None of the coaches caught him. None of the players turned him in.

Denny walked back into the screening room. "What happened?" he asked. If anyone outside of Wally Polk's closed office knew the details, Ernie Watson was sure to be the one. "He got caught, huh?"

Ernie glanced at the door while he continued to thread the film into the projector. He dropped his voice to slightly above a whisper. "Came in late, drunk," he said. "Osterman caught him."

Leon Osterman was a graduate assistant, working on an advanced degree in physical education. In return for free room and board at Burwood Hall, he was charged with seeing that the rules were obeyed. He seldom caught a violator. The players in Burwood Hall figured that Leon Osterman was either too nice, or too indifferent, or too blind and deaf to do the job. But this time he had caught someone.

"Finally, huh?" Denny said.

"Finally," Ernie agreed. "Seems that Osterman decided to run a bed check—nobody knows why, after all this time—at two o'clock in the morning, and Louie wasn't there. Osterman was sitting on the front steps waiting for him when Louie came toddling in. And that was that."

"Didn't take them long to decide what to do."

"My guess is that Coach Polk knew something was fishy—the old man knows everything—and he told Osterman to catch him."

"Umm," Denny said. He settled into a chair to wait for the coaches and the start of the screening.

22

He wondered where Louie St. Pierre was at this moment. Probably asleep in his room in Burwood Hall. He wondered if Louie knew yet that he was being suspended for a week. Probably not. He'd surely guessed that he was in serious trouble. But Leon Osterman did not have the authority to suspend him on the spot. So Louie probably went to bed without knowing. Denny wondered about Louie's reaction when he awoke to learn his fate. Probably a laugh, a wave, maybe a wisecrack—nothing more. Louie St. Pierre didn't worry about things. He just threw bull's-eye passes and won games.

Still, Denny did not consider the loss of Louie St. Pierre for one week to be a disaster for the Sutton State Cowboys. It was indeed fortunate—whether through blind luck or clever scheming—that the episode occurred this week and not last. The Allerton Lions, coming up this week, presented nowhere near the same threat that Gordon Tech had. The talents of Louie St. Pierre would not be needed, and Louie would hardly be missed. Besides the blessing of the schedule, there was John Porter. The Cowboys' second-string quarterback, understudy to Louie St. Pierre, had not been able to play last week. He was hobbling horribly on a sprained ankle. But he would be ready to step into Louie's shoes against Allerton.

Denny heard a door open. The voices from outside the screening room became clear. The familiar voice of Mackie Loren, the athletic publicity director, was saying, "I'll handle it and get back to you." Of course, Mackie had been in on the meeting. He had been brought in to prepare himself for the barrage of questions bound to come roaring in from the sportswriters and sportscasters all over the country, once the word of Louie St. Pierre's suspension got out.

Wally Polk, a huge mug of steaming coffee in one hand, led his assistants into the screening room. He was wearing cowboy boots, scuffed and dusty, along with faded jeans and a braid-trimmed cowboy shirt, his usual attire outside the glare of the public eye. He glanced at Denny. "Good morning, Denny," he said. He turned to Ernie. "Ready?"

"Yes, sir," Ernie said briskly.

Polk lowered his rangy frame onto a chair behind a small table, a pad of paper in front of him, and waited.

The assistant coaches nodded to Denny as they entered. Their faces, more than Polk's, seemed worried. Their expressions seemed questioning, as if they were asking Denny: Do you know yet?

But nobody said anything about Louie St. Pierre.

"Catch those lights, will you?" Polk said to no one in particular.

The room darkened, and the leaping, running, falling figures of football players filled the screen.

Burwood Hall, as usual on a Sunday afternoon, was quiet. Most of the players were gone. For a college

24

football player, Sunday offered the only real chance for social life during the weeks of the season. In the sitting room, a couple of players thumbed through the Sunday papers. Off to the side, another pair watched a professional football game on television, the volume turned low. Upstairs, along the corridor of the bedrooms, music and conversation could be heard. Again the volume was low. In some of the rooms, players sat at their desks, books open, studying.

Among the missing was Louie St. Pierre. He had arisen after lunch to hear—from whom, nobody seemed to know—the word that was buzzing by now through the whole dormitory: He was suspended for one week.

"He's probably at the library studying," somebody said, and laughed. Louie maintained a decent grade-point average but managed somehow to do so without the least evidence of effort.

"Maybe he's at the field house trying to talk the old man out of it," somebody said.

"That's as unlikely as having him at the library pounding the books," somebody else said. Louie St. Pierre never begged for anything.

The players all took the news in stride. They were interested but neither surprised nor worried. Louie had been asking for it. He had the punishment coming, and it was overdue. In the long run, his getting caught probably was for the best. Louie would shape up now. As for the Cowboys missing him against Allerton, well, for sure, Louie St. Pierre's talents would be missed. But John Porter would step in and quarterback the Cowboys to victory. There was nothing to worry about.

None of them recalled that bad news always comes in threes.

3

By the hour of practice on Monday, the Sutton State Cowboys' field house was swarming with reporters—from Dallas and Fort Worth, from El Paso, even from as far north as Denver. They were crowded into the lobby, trying to buttonhole players arriving for practice. They were drifting downstairs to the corridor leading to the dressing room, only to be chased back upstairs. After all, one of the nation's leading passers, the quarterback of one of the nation's top football teams, had been benched for a week for breaking training rules.

Denny walked through the crowd of reporters in the lobby unrecognized and skipped down the stairs, heading for the dressing room to change for practice.

Wally Polk kept himself in the dressing room, away from the prying eyes of the television cameras and the shouted questions of the reporters, until his players were dressed and ready to take the field. Then he stepped into the center of the dressing-room floor. He turned slowly, eyeing the players around him, until the conversations faded away into silence and everyone was watching him.

"As you all know by now, Louie has been suspended for a week," Polk said. The volume of his raspy voice was barely above the level of normal conversation. In the quiet of the room, he was easily heard. "Louie broke our training rules. He's got to pay the price. But so do we all. Louie will miss the Allerton game. We will work hard and win the game without him." Polk paused. Then he said, softly but distinctly, "There is no one player who is indispensable to a good football team."

At the back of the room, Denny sat next to John Porter. The Cowboys' number two quarterback sat motionless, staring at his tightly wrapped ankle. Then he began working the foot back and forth slowly.

Across the room sat Doug Stephens, the number three quarterback, a freshman with great prospects. Doug was watching John Porter slowly wiggle his bandaged ankle.

At the far side of the room, Louie St. Pierre, wearing a sweat suit, stood with arms folded across his chest, keeping his eyes on the coach. Although suspended, Louie was required to turn out for practice. He got no vacation for violating the training rules. He would spend his practice week jogging in circles around the field.

"Louie regrets his action now," Polk said. "We all do. But Louie understands the reasons for my decision. We all must understand the reasons, and we must simply move on from there."

Louie's face showed nothing. He did not seem angry or worried or remorseful or—and this was unusual for Louie St. Pierre—amused either.

Outside, heading for the practice field, Denny jogged past the coach and heard him tell a reporter, "Yes, yes, Porter will be able to play."

The reporter should have known already. Denny had read the word in the morning newspaper. The fact that John Porter would be healthy and ready for Allerton was high in Mackie Loren's original announcement.

Denny did not see the accident happen.

He was at the far end of the field, running his redshirts through their first simulation of the Allerton Lions' plays. George Coleman, the venerable chief scout of the Cowboys, was with them. He carried a large loose-leaf notebook, each page a crazy-quilt diagram of a football play. It was the "Allerton book," compiled on Sunday after Coleman had spent Saturday at some distant field watching the Lions in their last game. Between plays, he leaned into Denny's huddle with the notebook, specifying a play, passing the book around, demanding acknowledgment from all that they understood the thrust of the play coming up. Across from the redshirts, the Cowboys' first-string defense unit stood waiting to follow their coach's directions to block the play. The action was half-speed dummy scrimmage—no hard blocking, no tackling. It was the standard Monday dress rehearsal for the defense, the first step toward mastering the Allerton Lions' offense on the coming Saturday.

At the near end of the field, the Cowboys' offense units were running plays. One backfield crew worked with John Porter, limping slightly and moving slowly. Another backfield, with Doug Stephens at the helm, clicked off the same plays. They were working on timing. Behind the two backfields, Bucky Summers, the chief assistant coach for the offense, kept a watchful eye.

The first Denny knew that anything was wrong at the other end of the field was when he saw Ernie Watson break and run from his station at midfield. Then from the sideline Doc Reilly, the Cowboys' trainer, went puffing in at a half run. Somebody was down.

"C'mon," barked Coleman. "They'll take care of it. We've got work to do."

Denny ducked into the huddle. Coleman leaned in and called the play. Everybody got a glance at the book. Everybody nodded. Yes, they understood it.

"Okay," Denny said with a clap of his hands. "Let's go."

The play, in slow motion, sent a back past Denny on a fake into the middle of the line, followed by a pitchout around end.

Denny, whirling, sent the ball out to the racing back with a spiraling underhand toss. The ball had no more than left his hands when he turned back to look at the other end of the field.

Past the broad, squat form of Doc Reilly, Denny could see the figure of Doug Stephens, on his feet now, his face twisted in pain. Doc was doing something to Doug's shoulder. Doug was protesting. Wally Polk was approaching now, saying something to Doug, then turning to Doc with a questioning expression on his face. Doug, with Doc steering him, turned and walked off the field, headed for the dressing room.

Beyond them, Denny saw John Porter standing there watching, favoring his injured ankle even as he stood still. Off to the side, Louie St. Pierre, in his sweat suit, had quit jogging in a large circle around the practice field. He was standing and watching. The swarm of reporters, held off the practice field, trailed Doug and Doc down the field toward the field house.

Seeing Louie and John and Doug all in the same picture, Denny thought for the first time that the Sutton State Cowboys were running out of quarterbacks.

"C'mon, c'mon, let's get to work," Coleman called out.

Doug Stephens, with a shoulder separation, had gone to the hospital by the time the players trooped into the dressing room after practice.

31

"It was freaky, just plain freaky," Ernie Watson was saying. As usual, he was dispensing news bulletins with relish. The worse the news, the better Ernie liked it. "He was running. He had just handed off the ball. He didn't even have the ball. And he tripped over somebody's foot. Maybe his own. I don't know. He went down in a funny way. I just happened to be watching him at the moment. He went down in a funny way, just the wrong way, I guess, and he didn't get up."

Denny walked away from the group around Ernie and, with a towel around his waist, headed for the shower. The other players might have the time to stand around and listen to Ernie's detailed report. Denny had to hurry. He had a meeting with George Coleman in the screening room to go over some of the Allerton plays for tomorrow's practice, standard Monday procedure. The earlier they got started, the earlier they finished and he was free to go to Burwood Hall for his dinner.

Players were still straggling toward the showers when Denny, dried and dressed, scooped his notebook out of his locker and left for the screening room down the corridor.

"Is it bad?" Denny asked Coleman, when he walked into the screening room. "I mean, is Doug out for a while?"

Denny and the elderly coach had become good friends in their four years of working together. Cole-

32

man, who never saw the Cowboys play but always was somewhere else watching next week's opponent, viewed the redshirts as his team. As a result, Denny was his quarterback. Coleman seemed to see in Denny a quality rarely found in college football players—a scholar's view of the game—and Denny sensed the coach's fondness for him. George Coleman was a coach without a team that ever played a real game. Denny Westbrook was a quarterback who never played in a real game. They had an unspoken bond.

"I'm afraid so," Coleman said.

"That's too bad," Denny said. He sat down at the table, ready to go through the notebook with the coach. "With Louie being benched, Doug was sure to have gotten some playing time behind John."

Coleman glanced at Denny in a funny way. "You haven't heard?"

"Heard what?"

"John can't play either."

"What?"

"The doctors just looked at his ankle. It didn't hold up as well out there today as they had hoped. The swelling had gone down over the weekend. But now it's coming back. They think he's going to have to stay off the ankle for at least five days." Coleman watched Denny closely. "I thought you had heard."

"No, I—"

"It was all over the dressing room."

"I went into the showers ahead of the others,"

Denny said absently. "And then I hurried out to come in here. I didn't talk to anyone."

"They're both—John and Doug, both of them—out for the Allerton game."

Denny took a deep breath.

The week was beginning to look really crazy.

4

By the time Denny returned to Burwood Hall from the meeting with Coach Coleman, most of the players had eaten and left the dining room. Denny waved at a couple of them finishing up at a table against the wall. He walked to the counter, fixed himself a ham-and-cheese sandwich, and drew a large glass of milk from the dispenser. He carried his dinner from the basement upstairs to the sitting room.

Players were scattered around the room. Some were seated at a long, narrow table, poring over their books. They preferred studying in the company of others. The backdrop of conversation and noise was better than the stony silence of their bedrooms. At the card table, Tim Van Buren and the three other regulars, Mark Madison, Dan Graham, and Dutch Hauser, were continuing the world's longest bridge game. It had been going on for almost four years. John Porter sat alone, his crippled right ankle up on a bolster, staring at a television program.

On the sofa a newspaper lay open to a page showing the smiling face of Louie St. Pierre. Above the picture a headline announced the suspension of the quarterback for disciplinary reasons.

Louie St. Pierre was not in the room, which was probably just as well. Of the three sidelined quarterbacks, Louie alone was responsible for his being out of action. His misbehavior, not an unavoidable injury, had removed him from the lineup. When the Sutton State Cowboys, crippled and shorthanded at quarterback, faced the Allerton Lions on Saturday, only Louie St. Pierre could have made things different. If the championship, the national ranking, and the postseason bowl invitation went down the tubes because of that game, only Louie was to blame. Denny understood why Louie St. Pierre was not in the sitting room. He was in his bedroom upstairs, or out at a movie, or somewhere. He was anywhere but here with his teammates this evening.

Denny took a seat on the sofa, at an angle to John Porter's chair, and placed his sandwich and milk on the low table in front of him. "Sorry," he said. "Tough luck."

John looked around from the television screen. "Yeah, thanks," he said. "That's the way it goes, I guess."

"Heard anything about Doug?"

"He's spending the night at the infirmary. He'll be okay, but not by this weekend."

Earthquake Morrison walked in. He spotted Denny

and called out, "Hey, Flea! Are you ready for your big chance on Saturday?" Earthquake, an offensive tackle, enjoyed claiming—and loudly proclaiming— that the value of the quarterback to a football team was vastly overrated. Up front in the line, where Earthquake took bruises and dealt them out, that was where the games were won, to his way of thinking. Anybody could dance around at quarterback and hand off the ball or throw it to someone, if he had blockers up front protecting him. "All ready to go?" he repeated.

Earthquake was grinning. But nobody laughed. Nobody even smiled. At the card table, the bridge game came to a halt. At the study table, people looked up from their books. John Porter turned from the television set and looked at the others in the room. The question in the minds of all of them had finally been spoken.

"Did I say something wrong?" Earthquake asked.

"You always say something wrong," Dan Graham said.

"Aw, now, that's Louie's line. I thought all the rest of you guys agreed with me that the quarterback's not important." He turned to Denny. "No offense."

Denny, with a mouthful of ham-and-cheese sandwich, grinned at Earthquake. If Denny Westbrook had had any illusions about his quarterbacking abilities, he might have been angered or embarrassed. If he were anywhere near being a candidate for the job, he might have been hurt. But Denny had no illusions—privately or publicly—and everyone knew it. He swallowed his mouthful and said, "I don't come cheap, you know. Do you think you guys can afford me?"

"Seriously," Tim Van Buren said, "if not you . . . then who?"

Denny shrugged and recited the rhymes he had heard since his freshman year from the giants he played the game with, "Five-foot seven, headed for heaven." And: "One forty-five, not long to be alive."

Earthquake dropped into a chair near the door. "And never a word about your bullet passes, your dazzling runs."

"Right," Denny said. "Just jealousy, that's all."

Tim could not help smiling. But he repeated, "Then who?"

"Him," Dan Graham said, pointing to the door.

Everybody turned and looked.

Lamar Henry, with a notebook under his arm, stopped in surprise. "Huh?" he said. "I didn't do it. I was at the library. I have witnesses."

"You were a quarterback in high school, weren't you?"

"Oh," said Lamar, getting the drift of the conversation. He put his notebook down on a lamp table. Lamar Henry, like so many defensive backs in college football, had been a quarterback in high school. Frequently in high school the best athlete went to the quarterback position automatically. But in college,

38

where quarterback talent abounded, they found their niche at another position. Lamar was one of them. A junior defensive back, Lamar was the pillar of the Cowboys' secondary, the team leader in pass interceptions, a sure tackler. "Oh, no, not me, no way," Lamar said. "I haven't handled the ball on offense in more than three years."

"Somebody's got to do it."

Lamar looked genuinely alarmed. Obviously the thought of inserting Lamar Henry at quarterback on short notice never had occurred to him. "I've forgotten the words," he said. "What are they? Hut . . . hut . . . hut. Yeah, that's it. No, I've forgotten."

"He doesn't want to give up his skilled position to play quarterback," Earthquake said with a leer.

"That's it," Lamar said. "That's it exactly."

John Porter did not see the humor in Earthquake's remarks about the quarterback position. "Earthquake, that's exactly what you are—an earthquake, a disaster, a tragedy, a terrible act of God."

"I'll play quarterback then," Earthquake offered.

Nobody paid any attention this time.

"I think I know who it will be," Lamar said. "Mike O'Brien."

Mike O'Brien was what the sportswriters liked to refer to as a sophomore sensation. A flanker, he was the Cowboys' leading pass receiver. He had scored at least one touchdown on a pass in each of the Cowboys' games. He was an explosive runner, either with a pass or taking a pitchout around end. His speed, balance, and uncanny change-of-pace ability added up to big yardage almost every time he got his hands on the ball. Recruited from the same high school as Louie St. Pierre, he had played quarterback there in his junior and senior seasons following Louie's graduation. Louie had been a big factor in luring Mike to the tumbleweed country of Sutton State, and the two remained close friends. Denny hardly knew Mike. When Mike had arrived on campus the previous year, he was clearly bound for stardom. And equally clear, he knew it and so confined the pleasure of his company to others of star quality. This category did not include Denny Westbrook.

"That's right," Tim said. "Mike was an all-stater at quarterback, wasn't he? Same school as Louie. I'd forgotten."

Denny finished off the ham-and-cheese sandwich, took a long drink of the milk, and said, "You're forgetting one candidate."

"Who's that?"

"Louie St. Pierre."

The room was silent a moment. Then Tim said, "I don't think so."

Dan Graham said, "I don't either."

Lamar Henry said, "Coach Polk wouldn't go back on the suspension. He'd rather see us get whipped 60-0."

Dutch Hauser grinned and tilted his head to the

40

side slightly. "I don't know," he said. "It might not be such a bad idea."

"C'mon," Dan said. "The coach has got to maintain discipline. He doesn't have a choice in this one."

As Denny listened to the players convince themselves that the return of Louie St. Pierre was impossible, he came to believe that his suggestion was indeed possible. He had tossed in the name of Louie St. Pierre for no better reason than to see the reaction. But while the players protested, Denny's mind clicked down a list of facts. The Cowboys had to have a quarterback. Two of them were sidelined with injuries, and the other was out with a disciplinary suspension. Two other players—Lamar Henry and Mike O'Brien —had quarterbacking experience. But putting either of them at quarterback weakened the team at another key position. There was, among them all, only one who was able to play quarterback and able to do so without hurting the team elsewhere. That one was Louie St. Pierre.

"Yeah," said Dan, "I don't see how he could do it."

"Easy," Denny said. He had remained quiet during the flurry of comments. Now all heads turned toward him. "Really easy," he said. "Coach Polk simply announces that he is doing it for us—the boys who have worked and sweated and who deserve better than to lose just because one player went flooey and came stumbling in drunk after curfew. See, it's real easy."

"Man!" Dan said in disbelief.

"I never knew you were such a cynic," Tim said.

"It happens on the redshirts all the time," Denny said with a shrug.

"No way," Lamar Henry said. "You've about convinced me that it's—jeez—me or Mike O'Brien."

"No, I agree with Lamar," Tim said. "Coach Polk won't back off this suspension, not even if we have to take a 60-0 shellacking."

"Well, let me ask you this: Where is Louie St. Pierre right now?" Denny was leaning forward. His face was wearing a conspiratorial grin. He was enjoying himself. "Louie's not here, is he?" Denny waved an arm around the room. "He's not here. He's at the field house, I'll bet, being allowed right this minute to promise that he will never be a bad boy again."

The pay telephone in the corridor outside the sitting room rang.

"That's the press, trying to reach Louie for an interview right now," Denny said. "Mackie Loren has already put out the word."

The telephone continued to ring.

"Somebody answer that thing, will you?" John Porter said.

"I'll get it," Lamar Henry said. He was standing near the door. "But don't appoint me quarterback while I'm gone." He stepped through the door into the corridor.

Denny sat back, grinning. He was pleased. The deadly serious conversation was in turmoil. Nobody knew what to think. Nobody but Denny, that is. He was sure that Louie St. Pierre's suspension would be lifted. It was the only way. The Cowboys could not play without a quarterback. They could not afford to lose Lamar Henry's talents in the defensive secondary or Mike O'Brien's spectacular catches and dazzling runs by placing one of them in the now unfamiliar quarterback position. The stated reason for bringing Louie back might not be the one Denny had cited. But no matter what it was, there could be only one decision: Louie would have to come back. Denny Westbrook had not studied football from the sideline for four years for nothing. Louie St. Pierre would be back, simply because the team had to have him.

Lamar walked back into the sitting room. Everyone looked around questioningly. Lamar had not hailed somebody to the telephone with a shout up the staircase leading to the bedrooms. So the call was for one of them in the sitting room. Lamar looked at Denny. "It's for you," he said. Lamar had a funny look on his face.

Denny stood up. "Probably Coach Polk wanting my advice in this moment of crisis," he said. He walked out into the corridor and picked up the telephone.

"Hello."

"Denny?"

"Yes." The voice was vaguely familiar.

"This is Coach Polk, Denny."

"Yes, sir."

"Denny, you're it on Saturday."

Denny stared in silence at the instruction card on the pay-telephone box. The card told how to dial a long-distance call directly. There were a lot of numbers involved. The numbers faded into a blur in Denny's vision.

"Denny, you there?"

"Yes, sir. I'm here."

"Get a good night's sleep. And tomorrow morning, when you've got a break in your classes, come around to the field house. We've got a lot to talk about."

5

But Denny did not get a good night's sleep.

Upon hanging up the telephone, he stood for a moment, staring again at the lettering on the card explaining how to dial a long-distance call directly. The paint on the wall to the left of the telephone was chipped a bit. Denny had never noticed it before. And to the right of the telephone, in scrawled pencil, was a telephone number—255-2652. He wondered absently whose number it was. Maybe a sorority house. More probably, a pizza palace that delivered. Anchovies or pepperoni? Denny shrugged.

What now?

Denny could walk back into the sitting room and tell his teammates the good—or was it the bad?— news of Wally Polk's decision.

He could follow the directions on the card and dial his home in Louisiana directly and tell his father to be sure not to miss the Cowboys' game on television on Saturday. We've got a little surprise for you at quarterback.

He could call Paula and announce that her boy-friend was not, for once, going to be loitering on the sideline at this Saturday's game. Instead of sitting in the grandstand watching Denny, helmet in hand, strolling the sideline, she would be cheering him. Or more likely, Denny thought ruefully, she would be covering her eyes in horror every time he handled the ball. Denny glanced at his wristwatch: a few minutes after nine o'clock. He smiled. Paula Bradford was the one person in the world he could not tell at this particular moment. They had dated, more or less on a steady basis, for two years. But, as editor of the *Daily Cowboy Times*, Paula was first of all a newspaper-woman and secondarily Denny Westbrook's girl friend. At this hour of the evening, she would be at the newspaper office laying out tomorrow morning's front page. Denny's announcement, he knew, would be on the front page if he told her the news. Paula felt strongly about what she called "the people's right to know." "If you don't want me to print something, then don't tell me," she always said to Denny. So Denny decided not to call and tell her.

What now then?

He could call *Sports Illustrated* magazine in New York—again using the card for guidance on dialing long distance directly—and tell them to bring on their color photography crew for next week's cover picture. Or he could call Wally Polk back and tell the coach that he was crazy. But, being Denny Westbrook, he

46

hitched up his trousers, took a deep breath, and strode into the sitting room where the players were waiting.

"Coach Polk has decided to reject my advice," Denny announced.

Denny's eyes met those of Lamar Henry. Lamar had answered the telephone. Lamar knew the caller was Wally Polk. The knowledge had been conveyed in the puzzlement of his expression when he told Denny the call was for him. The look of puzzlement was still on Lamar's face.

By now, for sure, all of the players in the room knew from Lamar that the caller had been Wally Polk.

"C'mon, cut the jazz," Dan Graham said.

"What'd he want?" Tim asked. Tim looked as though he already knew the answer.

"I think. . . ." Earthquake Morrison said slowly, letting the statement trail off to nothing.

"I think so too," said Lamar Henry.

John Porter, turning in his chair, the bandaged ankle remaining on the bolster, stared at Denny without speaking.

"I admit that I was wrong," Denny said solemnly with a shake of his head. "Coach Polk will not call Louie St. Pierre back from Siberia for the Allerton game."

Denny waited, looking around the room. Nobody spoke. He dreaded the moment he had to confirm all their suspicions. He dreaded their reaction. But he put

47

a smile on his face. "He did not mention you, Lamar," he said, turning to look at the defensive halfback. "And he did not mention Mike O'Brien."

Earthquake broke into a wide grin. "We'll do it, little fella," he said. "We'll make a star out of you!"

"Good God!" Tim said. The words were barely more than a whisper. He was smiling at Denny.

"I have agreed to accept the assignment," Denny stated solemnly. He raised a hand for silence. "And now you must excuse me. My coach directed me to get a good night's sleep."

He bowed slightly to the ring of astounded faces and turned and left the room. He walked stiffly down the corridor to the staircase. He walked up the stairs, turned into the second-floor corridor, stepped off the twelve paces to his room, and went inside. He closed the door and—finally—exhaled. Then he turned on the light.

Denny looked around the room. There was Boogie Hadley's bed, unmade as usual. Boogie, the starting right guard on offense, had more bad habits than the rest of the team put together. On the field, however, he was undiluted terror and perfection as a blocker.

Above Denny's bed there was the picture of the red-shirt team. Denny was easy to spot in the crowd. He was a head shorter than anyone else. Next to it there was the picture of Denny in action on the practice field. It was, in truth, a funny picture. He was uncorking a pass. His weight was on the wrong foot. Both

48

arms were out straight and stiff. His facial expression was a hilarious mixture of confusion, hope, and dismay. Any quarterback—even Louie St. Pierre— might be caught on film at an awkward moment. But only Denny Westbrook would request a print for framing. He said he found the photograph reassuring. "It proves that I'm not as bad as I look," he said. "I couldn't be." But now, gazing at the image, he was only reminded that he was not anybody's idea of a picturebook quarterback.

Denny turned and looked at himself in the bureau mirror. A nice enough face, he decided. Perhaps the nose was a little long, like a beak, but he had a nice chin, a strong jaw. Then came the shoulders, broad enough, but thin. And the arms—muscular, but thin. No, not a picturebook quarterback.

But on Saturday, against the Allerton Lions, the figure in the mirror was the starting quarterback for the Sutton State Cowboys, number one team in the Southwestern Big Seven Conference, number five team in the national rankings, undefeated and untied.

Denny sat on his bed and stared into space. After a few minutes, in a soft monotone, he began reciting:

"Fact one: I cannot win with my strength and skill. There is little strength and little skill.

"Fact two: So I must win with my brains. I must win by thinking.

"Fact three: Earthquake Morrison says the quarterback doesn't matter anyway. Well, we'll see.

"Fact four: I don't know the Sutton State playbook well enough. I know the Gordon Tech plays—even the Allerton plays—better than I know our own plays. I must learn our plays. It will have to be the quickest study in recorded history.

"Fact five: Coach Polk thinks I can pull it off, obviously. I must remember that.

"Fact six: What have I got myself into?"

By the time Boogie Hadley arrived home the room was dark and Denny was piled up under the bedclothes, facing the wall. He heard Boogie ask, "Are you awake?" Denny, with his eyes wide open, said nothing.

Later, when Boogie was breathing evenly and the dormitory was deathly quiet, Denny slipped out of bed. He pulled on a robe. He looked at the glow of his wristwatch in the darkness: twenty minutes past midnight. Fumbling around on his desk in the darkness, he found his copy of the Cowboys' playbook, the loose-leaf binder containing his personal textbook of football, and a pencil. Tucking the books under his arm, he tiptoed out of the room, closing the door behind him.

When the first gray light of the early morning streamed into the sitting room on the ground floor of Burwood Hall, Denny took no notice. Seated at the long, narrow study table, a lamp at his left elbow bathing the area in light, he scribbled on a piece of

50

paper. Around him on the table were other pieces of paper scattered about. Some contained lists, neatly numbered. Others were marked with the x's and o's of football diagrams, copied and recopied from the playbook that had never before mattered, the one for the Cowboys' offense.

Denny leaned back suddenly and looked at the light coming through the windows. He felt a vague aching in his back. He looked at his wristwatch: 5:35. He yawned and stretched. Time to wrap it up. The kitchen help would be arriving any minute to prepare breakfast. He closed the playbook. Then he scooped up the loose sheets of paper, stacked them, and stuffed them into his loose-leaf binder. As he turned off the lamp he yawned again.

Upstairs, Denny dropped off the two notebooks at his room and walked to the showers at the end of the corridor.

The warm water of the shower and the comforting clouds of steam rising from the tile floor almost lulled him to sleep standing there. He lathered and rinsed, then gradually cooled the water until the needles coming out of the showerhead hit him like icicles. He woke up again.

Toweling off, shaving, and dressing quietly in his room alongside the slumbering Boogie Hadley, he felt fine. At least he told himself so. He wished he could quit yawning.

He was the first one in the dining room for breakfast, arriving at 6:15. The kitchen help, football fans all, greeted him with smiles and waves.

"You're up early," someone called out.

Denny wondered if they knew. Probably not. No, certainly not. How could they? He was relieved. This was one round of congratulations or consolations or whatever that he could delay. He was pleased to do so. This way he would enjoy his breakfast.

He downed a large glass of orange juice, walked upstairs to the front door and brought in the morning newspaper, and returned to the dining room to await the usual cereal, eggs, bacon, toast, and glass of milk.

The sports page was full of speculation about the Sutton State quarterback situation. The sportswriters had been quick to zero in on the fact that Lamar Henry and Mike O'Brien had played quarterback in high school. The sportswriters concluded that in a pinch—and the Cowboys were indeed in a pinch—either Lamar or Mike would serve as a logical choice. From there, they debated the merits of each—what was to be gained, what was to be lost—without coming to a conclusion. Also there was speculation that Louie St. Pierre's suspension might be lifted, given the extraordinary dilemma the Cowboys found themselves in. Buried deep in the stories was the word that Wally Polk was saying nothing. The veteran coach had not tipped his hand. Nowhere did the name of Denny Westbrook appear.

A small story, indented and boxed in with heavy

black rules, quoted the Allerton coach, Abe Thurman, "If Wally Polk needs a quarterback, I might be able to find one he could borrow." For the Allerton Lions, who had not defeated the Cowboys in six years, things were looking up. Clearly, the Allerton coach was a happier man these days.

Denny folded the paper and pushed it aside as the kitchen help began laying out the breakfast in huge trays on the steam table. He walked over, picked up a plate, and began helping himself.

Mike O'Brien came skipping down the steps and into the dining room. Denny turned and their eyes met. Mike, known for his early rising, was obviously surprised to see Denny already standing at the steam table. Equally obvious, Denny thought, was that Mike knew about Wally Polk's decision.

Mike stepped alongside Denny and picked up a plate. "I heard about it last night," he said with no preamble. "I couldn't believe it."

Denny blinked. Only Mike O'Brien, star of stars, sophomore sensation, could have—would have—said it. They are all thinking it, Denny knew, but Mike was the only one who would say so to Denny's face. In Mike O'Brien's mind, the world was composed of the great ones and the other ones, and everyone knew who was what. So why mince words?

"Thanks for the good wishes," Denny said.

"It's not like Polk didn't have any other choices," Mike continued, as if Denny had not spoken. "I could do it. So could Lamar." He paused. "I'd rather not. I guess Lamar would rather not too, but—"

Denny finished loading his plate and walked away from Mike in midsentence. He sat at the table where he had left the newspaper and hoped Mike would sit someplace else. Maybe someone else would come in, a friend of Mike's. But Mike followed Denny to the table and sat down. Denny knew that this was one breakfast he was going to eat in a hurry.

"Louie is all busted up about this," Mike said. "I was with him last night. He'd give anything not to have done what he did—getting himself suspended, I mean—and he'd give anything to be able to play on Saturday."

"Yeah, I guess so."

They ate in silence for a few minutes. Denny wondered how many of the players shared Mike's feelings. Sure, they all were surprised, Denny included. But how many of them—all of them?—agreed with Mike that anyone, Mike or Lamar, or even Louie, would have been a better choice? In the course of his busy night at the study table, the question had intruded itself on Denny's thoughts more than once. He wondered what the players in the sitting room had said after he marched out. Earthquake Morrison seemed to like the idea, or at least he was amused by it. Tim Van Buren, a friend, was pulling for him, Denny knew. But even Tim had been shocked. Doubtlessly, the whole world was going to be shocked when the word got out. But would the members of the Sutton State Cowboys football team accept the decision? That was the question.

Denny shoved his plate back and got to his feet. "Gotta go," he said. "See you later."

"Sure." Mike was reaching for the paper. "Sure, see you later."

Denny galloped up the stairs to the main floor two at a time. Then he took the stairs to the second floor two at a time. He grabbed the two notebooks off his desk, stuffed the pencil in his pocket, and started for the door. He stopped and stalled off Boogie Hadley, turning over, just awakening, and full of questions. "We quarterbacks have busy schedules," he said, and walked out.

The hour was still early, a few minutes before seven o'clock, and Denny had the campus to himself as he cut across on the familiar path from Burwood Hall to the field house.

There was no question about whether Wally Polk would be in his office at this hour of the morning. During football season, Wally Polk invariably could be found in one of three places— on the practice field in the afternoons, at the sideline of a football field on game day, and in his office in the basement of the field house the rest of the time. He viewed films—over and over and over again—in the early-morning hours, in the evening, in the late-night hours. He and his assistants met to chart strategy, discuss personnel, map practice plans, devise new plays at all hours. Wally Polk was a twenty-four-hour football coach in the autumn. No, there was no question about where Wally Polk was to be found at seven o'clock on this morning.

"But the question is," Denny said aloud with a slight grin as he pulled open the field-house door, "is Wally Polk ready for his first meeting with his new quarterback?"

The craziest week of Denny Westbrook's life was about to become the craziest week of everybody's life.

6

Wally Polk was standing next to his desk, a mug of coffee in his hand, glaring at a newspaper spread out on the desk, the same newspaper Denny had read while waiting for breakfast. It asked the questions: Lamar Henry at quarterback? Or Mike O'Brien? Or, maybe, Louie St. Pierre? The coach's jean jacket was hanging on a spoke on the wall. His cowboy hat was on a spoke next to the jacket.

There had been no one upstairs in the field-house lobby when Denny came in. There was no one in the row of darkened offices along the corridor. And there was no one in the coach's office except Wally Polk.

Polk looked up. "You're a little early, aren't you?" His face showed his surprise.

Denny smiled at the question. He enjoyed Wally Polk's surprise. He's not ready for me, he thought. He wasn't expecting me this early. The realization pleased Denny. A surprised and unready Wally Polk would be —in spite of himself—a more receptive audience for the ideas Denny was bringing in. This way, he hoped,

57

Wally Polk would do more listening than talking, and Denny would have a better chance of selling his strategy to the coach.

Polk glanced at his wristwatch. "Lord, it's only five after seven."

"I've been up all night."

Polk's right eyebrow shot up. "Oh?" he said.

Denny knew the meaning of the one-word question. He had observed—really, studied—Coach Wally Polk for four years. He knew what the arched eyebrow meant: trouble, alarm, a problem. Something was awry. There was bad news. In this case, the problem was obvious: The starting quarterback for Saturday's game with the Allerton Lions was already such a bundle of nerves that he could not sleep. And that, indeed, was trouble enough to arch the coach's right eyebrow.

"I've been working," Denny said, "and I've got some ideas." He dropped the two notebooks, the Cowboys' playbook and his own personal textbook of football, on the conference table next to the coach's desk.

"Oh?" Polk repeated. The tone was different, but the arched eyebrow stayed in place.

Denny shifted his weight from his right to his left foot. "The way I see it," he said, "we've got real problems going up against Allerton or anybody else with Denny Westbrook at quarterback. There's a lot of work to be done—you said so yourself—and there's no time to waste. So I stayed up all night working on the

58

problem." He stifled a yawn and managed a smile. "And, well, so here I am," he said with a shrug of the shoulders.

"You've got a plan," Polk said. He spoke slowly, as if trying to decide how to cope with a strange situation. The thought occurred to Denny that Polk, in all of his two decades of coaching, had probably never before had to acknowledge that someone else had a plan. Other people, especially players, did not tell Wally Polk how to plan for football games. He had not become a legend of college football and a giant on the national football scene by letting other people— especially players—lay out his plans for him. Wally Polk did the telling, not the listening, when the business at hand was a football game plan.

"I have a plan," Denny said. He spoke every bit as slowly and distinctly as Polk. He wore a wide grin on his face.

Polk studied Denny. The arched eyebrow went down. For a moment, Denny thought he saw a sparkle in Wally Polk's eyes. He half expected the coach to smile at Denny's obvious mimicry. With Denny Westbrook at quarterback, everyone might as well smile, Denny figured. Smiling was more fun than crying. But the sparkle in Polk's eyes, if it was there at all, vanished almost instantly.

"Okay, let's see what you've got," Polk said finally.

Denny peeled off his windbreaker jacket, tossed it over a chair, and he and the coach sat at the conference table, Denny at the head of it and Polk at his right elbow. Briefly Denny shuffled through the papers in his personal textbook of football. Polk barely glanced at the familiar playbook of the Cowboys. His eyes rested, with obvious curiosity, on Denny's book instead.

Denny looked up at the coach. "Let me say this at the outset, for what it's worth." He took a deep breath and looked Polk in the eye. "I want to win this game. This is the only game—the only game ever—in which I will play for Sutton State. I do not want to lose this game."

Polk watched Denny without moving or changing expression. "Just so we understand each other, young man," he said softly, "I never in my life went into a football game that I did not intend—and expect—to win, and I am too old now to change my ways."

Denny nodded. He thought that Wally Polk meant what he said.

Polk leaned back, draped a long arm over the back of the chair next to him, and crossed his legs. "Let me tell you something else," he said. He paused, seeming to weigh the words or perhaps wondering whether he was wise to speak at all. He stared past Denny, across the room for a moment, and then turned back to him. "If you quote me on this, if you tell a soul, I will call you a liar, and I may cut out your tongue for good measure."

Denny, puzzled, leaned forward slightly. He

expected a smile from Polk at the exaggerated threat. But there was no smile. Denny waited.

"We all—the assistant coaches and I— spent a lot of time last night kicking around our options. In the end, it came down to just two. Obviously, we could not repair John Porter's ankle. We could not fix Doug Stephens' shoulder. We could—and we considered the idea—put either Lamar Henry or Mike O'Brien in at quarterback. But there were good reasons not to move either of them. They're needed where they are. And, too, how good is a quarterback who hasn't played quarterback in three years? So we scratched those options. Either we lift Louie St. Pierre's suspension and welcome him back, or we don't. That's all. It was that simple. Or, putting it another way, it was a choice of Louie St. Pierre or Denny Westbrook."

Denny listened, trying to figure where Wally Polk was going with the line of conversation. Nothing so far surprised him. He knew the coaches could not heal John Porter and Doug Stephens. He knew the logic against switching Lamar Henry or Mike O'Brien to quarterback. He knew Wally Polk's reasons for not reinstating Louie St. Pierre.

"We voted," Polk said, "on whether to bring back Louie or go with you on Saturday. The vote was six to one, six in favor of bringing back Louie, and one in favor of saying that a suspension is a suspension and Denny Westbrook will be our quarterback," Polk paused. "You see, on this team I am a majority."

Denny stared at Polk. He was looking at a man who, against all advice, decided to cast his lot with Denny Westbrook. Denny could not blame the assistant coaches for their votes. From a team standpoint, their votes made more sense than Polk's. And from their own personal career standpoints, their sentiments were understandable. With their own records and reputations tied to the Cowboys' performance each Saturday, they wanted all the aces they could get in their hands. They wanted to take no chances. Wally Polk wanted the aces in his hands too. He wanted to take no chances. But Wally Polk was tougher than his assistants.

"I—"

"Now," Polk said, as if Denny had not started to speak, "what have you got there?"

By the time they had finished and Denny was stacking his notes and reinserting them in his personal textbook of football, the hour was approaching nine o'clock.

The assistant coaches had appeared, one at a time, early in the session. As each entered, Polk silently waved him to a seat and returned his attention to Denny's presentation. Each of the assistants, upon entering, cast a startled glance at Denny and a questioning glance at Polk. None of them said the words but they all asked by their expressions: What's going on here? The first of the assistants to arrive, and the most startled of all, was Bucky Summers, the chief assistant coach for the offense. Summers blinked at Denny, then nodded. Denny was, after all, Bucky Summers' quarterback for Saturday's game.

As for Denny, he could not help thinking as each of them entered the room: a vote for Louie St. Pierre.

But as Denny talked on while the minutes passed, the puzzled expressions on the faces of the assistant coaches changed to somber stares of intense concentration. They're listening anyway, Denny thought.

Now, his notes stashed away, Denny leaned back in his chair and waited.

Polk smiled slightly. "Very interesting," he said. He glanced around at the circle of his assistants. None of them said anything. "You'd better go on to class," Polk said.

Denny was hoping for something more. All through Denny's outline—almost a monologue—Polk had said little. He stopped Denny several times for questions but never offered an opinion, never a commitment. The assistant coaches said nothing. They leaned forward at several points—Bucky Summers more than the others—but they too offered neither opinion nor commitment. They were all going to hash out the points one by one after Denny had left.

Denny yawned widely. "I think I will go to bed instead," he said. "Chemistry and American history can live without me today." He glanced at his wristwatch. "I've had a long night." He paused and grinned. "Besides, how would it look if your quarterback fell asleep on the practice field this afternoon?"

As Denny was getting to his feet and reaching for his windbreaker, Mackie Loren came puffing into the room. "Coach. . . ." The Sutton State athletic publicity director stopped and stared at Denny. Then he gave a barely perceptible nod, as if suddenly grasping a fact. He turned to Polk. "The word is out—everywhere. I even got a call from the Dallas bureau of the AP. I didn't know what to tell them." He was pleading the eternal case of the publicity man who is quite often the last to know.

"Then I'm sure you sounded quite sincere when you pleaded ignorance," Polk said. He spoke gently. He and Mackie Loren had worked together for a decade, and they got along well. "I wanted to keep the world waiting for as long as I could."

"The players talk," Mackie said. "The word spreads like wildfire."

"I know," Polk said.

"I got a call from Austin Henderson, too." He glanced at Denny. Then he added, "He was trying to reach you. He did not sound happy."

Denny knew the name. Austin Henderson was a wealthy Houston oilman. He also was president of the Sutton Club, a Texas-wide organization of Sutton State graduates. The club was an important element of Sutton State's recruitment of outstanding high-school players all across the state every year. In

64

return, the club, in the person of Austin Henderson, felt privileged to offer advice on the football team. Denny had heard about the club almost from his first day on campus. He had read about the club in the newspapers and sports magazines. But Denny never had had any actual contact with it. He never had met Austin Henderson. Nobody had recruited Denny Westbrook for Sutton State. And once he was on the scene there, the Sutton Club had never inquired about his health or mood. They had never, during all his four years there, asked the first question about Denny Westbrook, as far as Denny knew. They never watched him when they visited the sidelines of the practice field. They did not even know who Denny Westbrook was, unless their eyes had happened at some idle moment to pass over his name far down the list of the football roster.

"I'm going to bed," Denny said with another yawn.

"Sure," Polk said. He nodded and waved a hand loosely at Denny while turning his attention to Mackie Loren.

As Denny walked out the door, his windbreaker over one arm and his two notebooks under the other, he heard Polk saying, "We will have an announcement at noon. You can tell them that, Mackie."

The first hint that Wally Polk was buying any part of Denny's plan came when Lamar Henry shook Denny into wakefulness.

65

"You've got a phone call—important, they said," Lamar kept repeating. "C'mon, roll out."

"What time is it?"

"Little after 1:30."

"Phone call?" Denny swung himself into a sitting position on the side of the bed, rubbing his eyes. He felt drugged. He had slept hard, dreamlessly. "Phone call, where?"

"Where do you think? At the telephone, downstairs in the hall."

Denny stretched his arms above his head. Then, barefoot and wearing nothing but his sleeping shorts, he padded out into the hall and down the stairs. He lifted the receiver dangling loose against the wall.

"Hullo."

"Denny Westbrook?"

"Yes."

"This is Abner Shell." Denny scratched his head. Then he came fully awake. Abner Shell was the head of the Broadcast Department in Sutton State's College of Communications. "Coach Polk called. He said to give you what you want. We're prepared to cooperate, of course."

"Oh," Denny said. "Oh, good. Yeah, that's great!"

"Just one thing," Shell said.

"What's that?"

"What is it that you want from us? Coach Polk didn't say."

66

7

After Denny hung up the telephone he stood for a moment, staring at the wall. There were the instructions for dialing a long-distance call directly. And there was that telephone number again: 255-2652. He rubbed the sleep out of his eyes. Then he smiled. He had it—the first bit of evidence that Wally Polk was buying at least a part of the plan. Denny wasn't crazy, after all. Or if he was, Wally Polk was joining him, and he was pretty good company.

Denny skipped up the stairs two at a time, walked past his room and into the lavatory, splashed his face with cold water, returned to his room, threw on his clothes, and rushed across the campus to the Communications building.

Abner Shell listened to Denny without interruption. His bewilderment was obvious. Apparently dumbfounded, he did not speak as Denny laid out the details of the request Shell had received from Wally Polk.

At the end, Abner Shell removed his glasses and replaced them. He studied his fingernails for a moment. Then he looked at Denny. "Really?" he asked.

"It's important," Denny said.

"I haven't even attended a football game since my own college days, and—"

"Can you do it?" Denny pressed.

Abner Shell shrugged. Then he smiled. "Sure, we can do it," he said. He reached for the telephone on his desk, punched four numbers, and asked, "Is Jerry Burton around?" After a moment, he said, "Jerry? Yes, can you come in for a minute?"

Denny never had met Jerry Burton, but he knew the name. Jerry, a senior broadcasting major, handled the evening newscasts on the campus radio station. Everyone knew Jerry Burton's name.

"Jerry will take care of you," Shell said. "And don't worry, all will remain confidential. Jerry is quite reliable."

Ten minutes later Denny was seated at a table in a small soundproof recording studio. There was a microphone in front of him. He held a piece of paper in his hand, one sheet taken from the notebook he had compiled during the long night at the study table. Across the table, Jerry Burton sat with a finger poised over a button on a tape recorder.

"Whenever you're ready," Jerry said. "After that, you restart each time my hand goes down. Got it?"

Denny cleared his throat, took a deep breath, licked his lips, and nodded. "Okay, now."

Jerry punched the button on the recorder. The reels began moving.

Denny said, "Normal three. Hut. . .hut. . .hut."

Pause. Jerry's hand dropped.

Denny said, "Quick-start three. Hut-hut . . . hut."

. Pause. Jerry's hand dropped.

Denny said, "Quick-finish three. Hut. . .hut-hut."

Over and over again, for more than twenty minutes, Jerry's hand rose and fell. Each time the hand dropped Denny recited combinations of the quarterback's snap signal, reading from the piece of paper in his hand.

"That it?" Jerry asked finally.

"That's it."

Jerry started rewinding the tape.

"I've got to have 'em—all of 'em—by seven o'clock in Burwood Hall. Okay?"

"No problem."

"Great. And thanks much."

"Sure. Think nothing of it."

The players were almost dressed for practice when Denny, breathing heavily after the jog from the Communications building to the field house, walked into the dressing room.

Mike O'Brien was tying a shoelace. Earthquake Morrison, already dressed out in his practice uniform, was in conversation with Hank Wilson, the offensive line coach. John Porter, wearing street clothes, was seated on a training table, his bare right foot extended, his trouser leg rolled up, getting a fresh taping on his sprained ankle. Doug Stephens, also in street clothes, his right arm in a sling, was chatting with Tim Van Buren while Tim pulled on his shoulder pads.

Outside in the corridor, Mackie Loren was shooing away one last reporter, promising, "There'll be a chance to talk later, but not here, not now. Please cooperate." The newspaper and television reporters had been swarming into town and over the campus since the noon-hour announcement. Denny, the object of all the activity, was such an unknown face that he had walked through a crowd of reporters in the field-house lobby and downstairs to the dressing room without being noticed. "Later, later," Mackie's voice rang out from the corridor.

Denny, his shirt almost off by the time he reached his locker, peeled his street clothes quickly and began pulling on his practice uniform.

Wally Polk came out of the coaches' dressing room, walked through the crowd of players without a word, and closed the dressing-room door, shutting off the final words of Mackie Loren's pleadings in the corridor. Polk turned and leaned his back against the closed door, surveying the players in front of him.

"Let me have your attention for a moment," he said.

After a brief stirring of players turning and stepping around lockers to get a view of the coach, the

70

room fell silent. Denny, with his shoulder pads in place but the practice jersey still in his hand, sat down on a bench and watched Polk.

"We're going to be doing some different things this week—and some different things on Saturday," Polk said. He was assuming that everyone in the dressing room already knew that John Porter and Doug Stephens, in addition to Louie St. Pierre, were out for the Allerton game. He was assuming too that everyone already knew that Denny Westbrook was the choice for quarterback. Denny figured the assumption was safe. The word had spread through the football dormitory and over the campus and into the town during the night. Through the morning the word—still unofficial —crackled over the long-distance telephone lines. And, since Mackie Loren's official statement at noon, the word had raced around the country, over the airwaves and into print. "Some *really* different things," Polk said flatly.

"Like playing without a quarterback," Mike O'Brien mumbled under his breath.

Denny, across from him, heard the remark. But he kept his eyes fixed on the coach. He did not change expression.

"Right now," Polk continued, apparently unaware of Mike's softly whispered aside, "the important point is this: nobody outside the circle of this football team is to know what we're doing. Nobody—not your girl friend, not your best buddy, not your parents back home. Nobody." He paused, glancing around the room. "Even among yourselves, be careful when you're speaking about our plans. Don't talk on the practice field where you might be overheard. Don't talk at a table in the student union, where somebody at the next table might hear you." He stopped for a moment. "And understand this: We don't even want anyone to know that we're doing anything special at all. Do you understand?"

Earthquake Morrison's husky whisper could be heard in the silence of the dressing room. "I think he means top secret."

Polk heard Earthquake and glared at the huge offensive tackle without speaking.

"Sorry," Earthquake muttered.

Polk ignored the apology. He continued, "Out there on the practice field today—and tomorrow and Thursday—it's business as usual, with Denny Westbrook, our best quarterback, at the controls." He paused. "It's business as usual," he repeated. "Nothing's changed. Understand?"

He waited, letting the point sink in.

Nobody spoke.

"There will be a meeting of the entire offensive unit in the basement of the dormitory, in the cafeteria in Burwood Hall, at eight o'clock tonight. There will be another meeting tomorrow night. And another one on Thursday night. If you've got plans, cancel them. Get out of it somehow. Don't say it is a team meeting. Say anything you like—I don't care what—but be there, and be on time. And wear tennis shoes."

Tennis shoes? All around the room the players shot puzzled glances at each other.

Except Denny. He shifted his gaze from the coach to the concrete floor of the dressing room, and he smiled. Wally Polk had decided to buy another part of Denny Westbrook's plan. Maybe the coach was buying all of it.

Denny turned the corner in the corridor outside the dressing room and shoved open the heavy door leading to the path to the practice field. He saw Polk surrounded by reporters.

"We've got one quarterback suspended for violations of the rules, and we've got two quarterbacks injured," Polk was saying. His voice carried the exasperated tone of one explaining the perfectly obvious for the umpteenth time. "When the first three quarterbacks are out, you play with the fourth-string quarterback. It's as simple as that. Can't you understand?"

"Is that him?" one of the reporters asked, pointing at Denny, whose small frame appeared swallowed up in the huge shoulder pads.

Denny turned and continued to walk toward the practice field. The reporters swarmed around him. Denny cast a questioning glance at Wally Polk. A television newsman with a minicam unit mounted on his shoulder moved over in front of Denny, the lens aimed squarely at his face, blocking out Polk.

"How does it feel?" somebody asked.

Denny grinned. The question seemed pretty dumb. "Same as yesterday," he retorted.

"What do you think—I mean, about being named the starting quarterback for the Cowboys on Saturday?" the questioner asked.

The television camera was whirring in Denny's face.

"I think," he said, and he paused, amused by the sight of everyone in the circle holding their breath while they waited for the momentous statement. "I think that being the starting quarterback on Saturday means that I had better get to practice."

Denny turned and jogged toward the practice field, leaving them behind.

Briefly his gaze met Wally Polk's. The coach seemed to nod slightly.

Behind him, Denny heard one of the reporters say, "Hey, isn't that Louie St. Pierre over there?" Denny did not turn to look. He continued his jogging stride toward the practice field.

"Business as usual on the practice field," Wally Polk had said.

But with Denny Westbrook at quarterback instead of Louie St. Pierre or even John Porter or Doug Ste-

74

phens, the practice session was anything but usual for the Sutton State Cowboys.

The offense, under the watchful eye of Bucky Summers, ran the plays in dummy scrimmage against a defense comprised of Denny's redshirt teammates. The plays were the same as always for the Cowboys' offense: pitchouts to the flankers, Mike O'Brien and Richie Carson; hand-offs to the fullback, Mark Madison, plunging into the middle of the line; sideline passes to Tim Van Buren and Mike O'Brien; quick passes over the center to the tight end, Andy Sterling; even a few quarterback keepers, a deadly effective play for the Cowboys when Louie St. Pierre was at the helm. They ran all the standby plays that had kept the Sutton State Cowboys at the top of the Southwestern Big Seven Conference and high in the national rankings for more than a decade.

But the plays didn't work. The plays that clicked with spectacular success in the hands of Louie St. Pierre went wrong for Denny. His passes, far from being bullets hitting the bull's-eye, wobbled and missed the mark. Mike was putting on the brakes and reaching back for passes falling behind him. Tim was lunging for overthrown passes. Denny's pitchouts lacked the zip that a runner likes to feel taking in the ball. Richie was bobbling the floating pitchouts. Denny's hand-offs were too high, too low, too late, too early. Mark, time and again, was still juggling the misplaced ball when he hit the line.

Furthermore, Denny's unfamiliarity with the Cowboys' plays—and his unfamiliarity with the players themselves—was taking a terrible toll. Never in four years had Denny quarterbacked a team out of the Cowboys' playbook. Always before he had quarterbacked out of the scouting report of another team's plays. True, Denny was used to working each week with a strange set of plays. The Cowboys' plays were no stranger to Denny than the plays he faced in any of the previous weeks. But he lacked the background, the deeply ingrained knowledge of the playbook, that a first-string quarterback always must possess.

Never in four years had Denny had the likes of Mike O'Brien and Tim Van Buren going out for his passes, or Richie Carson racing around end for his pitchouts. Always before Denny was feeding the ball to players with severe limitations—poor players, slow runners, whose shortcomings Denny had come to accept and accommodate. And his redshirt teammates too had come to accept and accommodate Denny's shortcomings. But the stars of the team were something else.

More than once Denny fumbled the snap from center, stopping the play before it got started. He and the center, Dutch Hauser, had never worked together. Uncertainty between center and quarterback leads to the worst of all happenings: a fumble.

Dutch, probably more than any player on the field, felt the difference in the quarterbacking, the difference between Louie St. Pierre, slick and accomplished, and Denny Westbrook, juggling and fumbling the ball. He said nothing, but Denny could not miss the look of disgust on his face every time Denny bobbled the ball, however slightly.

Through it all, Louie St. Pierre, wearing a sweat shirt and football shoes, jogged in monotonous circles around the practice field. Louie had been nowhere in sight at the brief team meeting in the dressing room before practice. Whether his absence was a result of Louie's own indifference or of Wally Polk's decision, Denny did not know. Now Denny could not help noticing the tall figure as Louie made his rounds.

He was also aware of being the focus of all eyes when Louie's jogging brought him past the floundering offensive unit at the south end of the field. Everybody—players and onlookers alike—seemed interested in Denny's reaction. With a conscious effort, Denny kept his eyes straight ahead and his mind on the business of the drill.

Once Louie stopped and, standing leisurely with arms folded across his chest, an amused smile on his face, watched the Cowboys run a play. Somebody called out a greeting to him, and he waved in reply. Bucky Summers turned, said something, and waved Louie on his way.

The fumbles, the missteps, the misplays, the poor timing, the errors resulting from not knowing the plays well enough, all weighed on Denny as the practice session wore on. His confidence began to ebb. Things were going even worse than he had feared. His plan, drawn up during the long night at the study table in Burwood Hall, seemed now to be a silly and futile scheme. How had he ever been able to sell any of it—perhaps all of it—to Wally Polk? Even the best plan required a minimal amount of execution for success. And Denny was falling on his face every time.

The encouraging words of his friends only made things worse. When Tim Van Buren said, "My fault," after dropping a poor pass, Denny flinched. The incompletion was not Tim's fault. It was the fault of the quarterback who failed to deliver the ball properly. When Mark Madison, trying to be helpful, explained where he wanted a hand-off placed, Denny felt like a kindergarten boy playing his first sandlot game. Through it all, Bucky Summers' faced showed nothing. He neither smiled nor frowned, and he seldom spoke as he guided the backfield through the routine of the drill. "Yes, yes," Denny told himself, when his eyes met those of the chief assistant coach for the offense, "I know the vote: six to one."

Mike O'Brien, quite unwittingly, was the one who snapped Denny back on track near the end of the practice session. They were in the huddle. Denny, on one knee, was leaning into the circle. He was preparing to call the play. To his right, Bucky Summers was leaning in, listening.

"Well, Polk said it was going to be different this

week," Mike muttered. He had just taken a hard dive to the ground in a frantic lunge for one of Denny's errant pitchouts. "And it sure as hell is different."

Nobody spoke. Mike's words hung in the silence for a moment. Then Denny turned his head slowly and looked up into Mike's face. "Shut up!" he said.

"What?"

"You heard me. I said shut up. I'm the quarterback, and this is my huddle. So shut up or get out of here."

Mike blinked at Denny in amazement. Denny kept a glare fixed on Mike, daring him to utter one more word. Mike said nothing. Nobody said anything. The huddle was deathly quiet.

Denny turned away from Mike to call the play and found himself facing the wide grin of Earthquake Morrison. "Butterfly left, on three," Denny said, clapping his hands together. "Let's go."

If Bucky Summers' expression varied in the slightest during the sharp interchange, Denny did not know it. He kept his eyes straight ahead as the players broke the huddle and lined up for the play.

"What's up?"

Tim Van Buren asked the question as he dropped into a seat alongside Denny at one of the cafeteria tables in the basement of Burwood Hall. All around them in the large room the members of the Sutton State Cowboys' offensive unit, more than thirty strong, were gathering. They stood in groups chatting, or they sat at the long tables speaking softly. The conspiratorial nature of their gathering, a secret meeting, left even the noisiest of the players in a subdued mood. No one but the players was in the cafeteria. The kitchen helpers, expressing surprise that everyone had finished eating so early, had cleaned up and gone, happy about the quick departure and asking no questions.

Denny grinned at Tim's question. "You'll see," he said.

Tim had better reason than most to know that something unusual was in the offing and to ask about it. In the crowded dressing room after practice, Tim had been the only player who had heard Wally Polk's casually stated remark to Denny, "I'll call on you to explain it tonight." Polk had come walking down the row of lockers where Denny and Tim and the others were dressing. He hardly slowed his stride as he spoke. He might have been saying, "See you later," or "Nice weather we're having." Denny had looked up at the coach, startled, and nodded his acknowledgment. There had been no time to answer. Polk walked on. Tim eyed Denny questioningly but, with the other players around, said nothing.

"What's in the cartons?" Tim pressed. "Our secret weapon?"

Denny glanced at the stack of cardboard cartons on the floor against the wall. They had been there waiting for him when he returned to Burwood Hall from practice.

"Yeah, that's it," Denny said. He smiled at Tim again. "Yeah, our secret weapon."

Tim waited a moment. Then when he realized that Denny was not offering a preview of what was to come, he shrugged and said, "Well, you've always said you wanted to be a coach, and now you're beginning to act like one—mysterious, man, mighty mysterious."

Denny grinned at Tim and said nothing. He yawned and stretched. The short nap had helped, but the sleepless night at the study table in the sitting room was catching up with him. It had been a long day.

Polk's casual announcement to Denny in the dressing room had come as a surprise. Coach Wally Polk never called on his assistants, much less his players, to outline important material. He always did the job himself. He was the head man of the Sutton State Cowboys. Nobody ever was to doubt who laid the plans, made the decisions, issued the orders about the way the Sutton State Cowboys were going to play football. But now he was saying that Denny Westbrook was to sketch the plan, explain the strategy, tell the team the tactics designed to bring victory over the Allerton Lions on Saturday.

For Denny, the surprise lasted only a few minutes. Wally Polk's logic was clear. That the plan was devised by Denny had nothing to do with it. That the team needed to accept Denny as the quarterback and the offensive leader and needed to accept him quickly had everything to do with it. Wally Polk was changing one of his immutable rules to meet an extraordinary situation. He was, in one fell swoop, placing Denny Westbrook in the leadership position, in fact as well as name.

Later, while Denny was walking from the field house to the dormitory, the full impact of Polk's one simple statement hit him: The coach was buying the deal, the whole deal, the entire scheme, all of it, without reservation. There was no selection among Denny's suggestions—okay on that one, nix on this one, maybe on that other one. He had said simply,

"I'll call on you to explain it tonight." The whole thing.

By the time Denny reached the front door of Burwood Hall and stepped inside, his mind was racing. The details of the plan, concocted at the study table in the early-morning hours, were clicking by in rapid succession. His heart was pounding. He could not wait to reach his room, turn on the light, close the door, and open the notebook. He had to organize his presentation.

The long, weary night of planning was worth it. The dismal performance on the practice field—the wobbly passes, the floating pitchouts, the badly placed and ill-timed hand-offs—were pushed to the back of his mind. Mike O'Brien's remark in the huddle was only a faded memory. Dutch Hauser's glares of disgust were no longer there. Bucky Summers' obvious reservations about Denny Westbrook as a quarterback no longer mattered.

None of it was going to matter if—*if*—the plan worked.

There was a bustle of movement at the door. The coaches, led by Wally Polk, entered. The assistants took seats at tables. Polk strode to the front of the room. He took up a position near the stack of trays where the players headed into the line to get their meals.

83

Polk glanced around the room. He seemed to be counting noses. Or maybe he was making sure that nobody but his players was in the audience. "Get that door, somebody," he ordered. Somebody got up and closed the door.

"I told you that we were going to do some different things this week, and they start right now," he said.

The players shuffled slightly and glanced at each other. Denny sat motionless, listening and watching, his hand resting on his ring-binder notebook. His mouth went dry. He had sold Polk on the plan. Now he had to sell the players.

"First, I am going to call on Denny Westbrook to outline the essentials of our plan," Polk said. "It's Denny's plan, and he will explain it. Then we'll go to work on it."

All around the room players straightened in their seats with startled expressions on their faces. They knew as well as Denny that Wally Polk always did the talking when the subject was important. Never was Louie St. Pierre called on to explain the strategy. And now Denny Westbrook. Denny Westbrook? A murmur of a dozen whispers filled the room.

"Let's have it quiet!" Polk snapped. "Okay, Denny."

Denny got to his feet, hesitated a moment, and then picked up the notebook and walked to the front of the room. He laid the notebook on a table in front of him and looked out at the faces staring up at him. Tim was

84

staring soberly at Denny. Earthquake was grinning. But most of the players had not yet recovered from their surprise.

"We've got a problem this Saturday," Denny said. "I am going to be your quarterback."

Nervous laughter rippled across the room. Denny grinned back at the players. Earthquake clapped his hands together in loud approval of the remark until he spotted Wally Polk glaring at him. Tim continued to watch with a blank face.

Denny's eyes met the unsmiling stare of Mike O'Brien. Mike was sitting next to Dutch Hauser. Dutch was not smiling either. Denny had a difficult time holding the grin on his face. Beyond Mike and Dutch, Denny saw John Porter and Doug Stephens sitting together at the rear of the room. They were not smiling. The face of Louie St. Pierre was nowhere in sight.

Through Denny's mind danced the thought, Yesterday I couldn't play on the same field with these guys, and today I'm their leader. He regretted allowing the observation to come to the surface. There was no time, no place, for that sort of thinking.

He took a deep breath. "I think that the things I'm going to suggest are logical—a little unusual, maybe, but logical—and I hope you'll agree with me that they will help," he said.

The room was deathly silent. The faces, all turned to Denny, were serious.

"And," he continued, a half grin appearing on his face, "if you think that what I'm suggesting is goofy, well, just remember that having Denny Westbrook at quarterback is pretty goofy in itself, and maybe we need some goofy things to make it work."

Some of the players exchanged glances. Denny took another deep breath and shifted his feet. "As I see it," he said, "the problem can be broken down into parts —a part that we have to work to overcome and a part that we can turn to our advantage. The problem we have to overcome is having a fourth-stringer at quarterback. The part that we can turn to our advantage is, well, some surprises."

Denny gestured at the cartons stacked on the floor against the wall. "There's part of our secret weapon," he said. He expected the heads in the audience to follow his gesture and look at the cartons. Most of the players, however, kept their eyes on Denny. "Those cartons contain tape recorders—one for each of you —and tape cassettes—one for each of you. The music on the tapes is me, calling the signals." He paused. "Any new quarterback, even if he's the greatest in the world, is a problem because his cadence is different. If you'll listen to the tapes in all your spare time between now and Saturday, well, I hope that my cadence will be so familiar to you that you'll be able to say it in your sleep."

Denny stopped and stepped back, thrusting a hand

into a hip pocket. "There's more to the tapes than familiarizing yourself with my cadence. We've got some long—really long—counts and some stutter counts in there. You see, Allerton knows we have a strange quarterback calling the signals. They will be expecting short counts. That's the usual thing with a new quarterback—a short count to minimize the chance of somebody jumping off side in anticipation of a strange cadence. So we'll go long with the count and try to make *them* jump off side." He paused. "Any five-yard penalties will come in handy."

Denny opened the ring-binder notebook on the table in front of him and glanced down the handwritten list on the page. "We've got to surprise them," he said softly, his face still down, staring at the page. Then he looked up. "And I think we can do enough of it—surprising them—to beat them."

Denny looked at the faces in front of him. Even Mike O'Brien appeared interested. "At certain points in the game, we will call two plays at one time in the huddle." He paused to let the words sink in. There was nothing revolutionary about calling more than one play in the huddle. Most teams were ready to do so to save time when victory was on the line and the final seconds were ticking away. But few teams— Denny knew of none—used the tactic as an offensive weapon. For the offense to line up and start a play without a huddle deprived the defense of the time to regroup and set their own signals. A confused defense offered enormous opportunities for the offense.

Denny explained his reasoning, and added, "This way, too, they'll never know in advance whether we're going to huddle. They'll never be sure of how much time they have to set their defense." He grinned. "With luck, we can panic them."

There were some nods in the audience. A couple of players turned and whispered something to a seatmate.

Denny pointed at Mark Madison. "Mark, you were a punter in high school, weren't you?"

The fullback nodded, puzzled.

"Can you quick kick?"

Mark shrugged. "Sure, I guess so."

"In my four years at Sutton State, and maybe in the forty years before that," Denny said, "the Cowboys never have quick kicked. The Cowboys are an explosive offensive team, always have been. The quick kick is the weapon of a defensive team. The Cowboys never have used the quick kick, never needed it." He paused. "Well, folks, we're not going to steamroller anybody on Saturday, and let me be the first to tell you. So let's quick kick once or twice. It'll drive them back, and it'll drive them crazy."

Mark nodded again.

Denny pointed at Mike O'Brien. "Mike, you were a quarterback in high school—an all-stater."

Mike, frowning, nodded slightly.

"But have you ever thrown a flanker pass at Sutton State?"

Mike shook his head.

"I know you haven't," Denny said. "And Allerton knows you haven't. With Louie St. Pierre at quarterback, who needed it? But with Denny Westbrook at quarterback, we need it. So let's do it."

Tim Van Buren was grinning broadly now. So was Earthquake Morrison. Even Mike O'Brien's scowl had softened. Wally Polk continued to stare at Denny without changing expression.

"We've got a couple of other things going for us," Denny said. He grinned. "One of them is looking bad in practice. I do it quite well. Maybe Allerton will be overconfident by Saturday. And the second thing we've got going for us is Sandy Ruzzo."

The Cowboys' little field-goal kicker rolled his eyes to the ceiling in mock alarm. He knew the burden on his shoulders. Short of quarterback power, the Cowboys were sure to be calling on him more than ever for a three-pointer when the offense was unable to punch its way into the end zone for a touchdown.

"If you have any questions," Denny said, "just speak up. I have all the answers in this little notebook entitled 'Tactics for the Hopeless.'"

Some of the players grinned as Denny picked up the notebook and returned to his seat at the table next to Tim Van Buren.

Polk moved back to his position near the stack of

trays. "Okay, first let's get these tables folded up and stacked back against the wall," he said.

As they were getting up, Tim leaned over to Denny and said, "You didn't guarantee victory."

Denny smiled briefly. "You noticed."

Denny awoke the next morning to the sound of his own voice, "Double-quick four: hut-hut . . . hut-hut."

Boogie Hadley was pulling on his jeans and stuffing in his shirttail in the dim morning light of their room in Burwood Hall. On the desk, the tape recorder, turned low, was broadcasting the quarterback's cadence, as spoken by Denny Westbrook. Boogie Hadley, an offensive guard, was doing his homework.

Denny turned over in bed without speaking and stared at the wall. He was comfortable in the bed and did not want to get out. Although he was no longer tired, he wished he could stay in the bed all day. The weariness was gone. That wasn't the problem. But he had awakened with a feeling of fright—a chilling fear —that would not go away. And the bedclothes protected him.

A question swirled around and around in his mind and would not go away: What if it doesn't work?

What if?

What if Boogie Hadley and all the others listened to the taped snap signals until they could say them in their sleep, and the familiarity didn't help? On the field, in the excitement of the game, he could mis-speak in his nervousness. The players wouldn't have the tape recording on the field. They would just have Denny Westbrook.

What if the center, Dutch Hauser, and Denny and Mark Madison did perfect the quick kick in the confines of the basement cafeteria, and it didn't work? Denny, overanxious, might tip the play to the opponents by lifting his hands too quickly. Or he might lift his hands too slowly, blocking Dutch's snap between Denny's legs to the waiting Mark Madison.

What if Denny's pitchouts to Mike O'Brien were off the mark or so wobbly that Mike couldn't get a handle on the ball in time to throw the halfback pass? It had to work the first time. That was the only time the play would have the element of surprise. What if it didn't work?

What if somebody—anybody—got mixed up when Denny called two plays in the huddle? A missed signal could mean an off-side penalty. Instead of a big gainer, the Cowboys could lose five yards to the penalty. A misunderstanding—somebody going the wrong way—could mean a fumble. Instead of a big gainer, the Cowboys could lose possession of the ball. What if?

92

What if Denny's plan failed to move the Cowboys into the range of a field goal by Sandy Ruzzo? Some offense was needed—at least a little—to get the Cowboys down inside the thirty-yard line, where Sandy needed to be for the odds to dictate success.

What if? What if?

The question seemed locked in Denny's brain. It had been there when he awakened. Now it would not go away. Where had the question come from, anyway? Denny had suffered not the least doubt during the long night at the study table, mapping out his plan. He was confident then that the plan would work. Why not now? He had stumbled through the practice session without doubts. After all, what the Cowboys were doing on the practice field was not what they were going to do on the field against the Allerton Lions. Also, looking bad on the practice field was part of the plan. The word would spread, and the Allerton Lions—if the Cowboys were lucky—would succumb to an advanced case of overconfidence. Even more important, the dismal practice sessions on the field helped to hide the secret work in the Burwood Hall basement cafeteria. There were no doubts in Denny's mind either, when he stood before the team in the cafeteria and outlined his plan.

So why now?

The drill in the cafeteria, lasting nearly two hours, had gone well. On one side of the room, Denny and

Mark and Dutch went through the ritual of the quick kick time and time again. Dutch bent over the ball, his huge hands wrapped around it. Denny crouched behind him in the quarterback position. Mark took the stance of the running back, ready to spring forward for a hand-off or to meet a blocking assignment. He stood directly behind Denny, four yards back.

The tape recorder called the signals. Denny mouthed the words with it, rehearsing himself in his own cadence.

"Okay, the next one," Denny said.

Then from the tape recorder, "Quick-start three: hut-hut . . . hut."

At the instant of the third "hut," Denny lifted his hands slightly off Dutch's rump, and Dutch sent the ball spiraling through Denny's legs to Mark's waiting hands. Mark kicked through, pulling the ball to the side in his right hand at the last moment.

The kick itself, the foot meeting the ball, needed no practice. Mark Madison knew how to punt. Getting the ball from Dutch through Denny's legs to Mark was another matter. So they went through the motions over and over and over again. In the end, Mark was smiling. Even Dutch acknowledged, "It works."

Across the room, a dozen offensive linemen in a row slipped into their three-point stance, listened to the clipped cadence being broadcast by the tape recorder, and, on signal, charged one step forward. At

first, they were a ragged row. They broke too quickly—
or too slowly. In a game, their miscues would mean an
off-side penalty or a missed block. So they practiced
over and over and over again. Gradually the line of
bodies began to move as one.

"Yeah, that's the way," Hank Wilson finally said.
The offensive line coach was watching from one end
of the row of linemen. "Once more now."

Behind the linemen, backfield players followed the
forward motion. Listening, they took one step at the
snap signal.

Bucky Summers took the ends and Mike O'Brien to
one side. Chalking on a blackboard, he diagramed the
flanker pass play, a play that was nowhere in the thick
playbook detailing the complexities of the Cowboys'
attack. Mike listened, frowning, as Summers identified
primary and secondary receivers and marked the
movements he expected the Allerton defense to make.
Tim Van Buren, designated the primary receiver,
smiled and nodded.

At the end of the session, with the other players
drifting upstairs to study or visit in the sitting room or
go to bed, Bucky Summers called out to Denny and
Dutch. "Over here," he said.

Denny knew what was coming. Obviously, from his
expression, so did Dutch.

Summers made no mention of the fumbled snaps
from center on the practice field. He simply told them,

"There is nothing more important than the transfer of the ball from the center to the quarterback. That is the point at which every offensive play begins. If it's screwed up, nothing can work."

So for thirty minutes, with the tape recorder calling the signals, Dutch snapped the ball to Denny's waiting hands, and Denny, coming out of the crouch, turned —first left, then right—in simulated hand-offs.

"Okay," Summers finally said. There was a note of resignation in his voice. Denny remembered that the vote had been six to one. "That's enough for tonight."

Upstairs, Denny scanned the corridor bulletin board. It was jammed with notices as always: telephone messages, club meeting notices, urgent pleas for a ride to Dallas or Houston or El Paso, newspaper clippings about the team, the now tattered and frayed list of dormitory and training rules.

The scrawled note hung by one thumbtack: "Westbrook—Paula."

"Yeah," Denny said aloud, nodding his head. "Yeah, Paula."

He walked to the pay telephone, dropped in coins, and dialed the familiar number of the Tri Delt house. By this hour, Paula would have put tomorrow morning's paper to bed and would be back at the sorority house.

"Why didn't you tell me?" she asked.

"Because you told me not to."

"What do you mean?"

"You've always said, if I don't want you to print it, then I shouldn't —"

"Okay, okay, I asked for that one. But why didn't you call me today, after the announcement?"

"I've been sort of busy. You can't imagine."

"We're always busy, both of us."

For Paula and Denny, the romance of the last two years had been confined—to an incredible extent—to the telephone, especially during football season. With Paula in journalism school and Denny majoring in physical education, their paths never crossed in the classrooms or the corridors. All through the school year, Paula's duties at the *Daily Cowboy Times* kept her tied up until late hours on the five week nights. And Denny's football responsibilities locked him in on the afternoons during the fall and during the period of spring drills. They enjoyed their Sundays together, but little more.

"It's been a busy day, believe me," Denny said.

There was a pause. Then Paula asked, "What's going on?"

Denny recognized the change in the tone of her voice. He no longer was speaking with Paula Bradford, his girl friend. He was speaking with Paula Bradford, the editor of the *Daily Cowboy Times*. She was Paula the reporter now.

He played it straight. "Well, Louie got himself sus-

97

pended, you know, and John got a bad report from the doctor, and —"

"That's not what I mean. I know all of that."

Denny was grinning into the telephone. Of course, she knew all that. "Then what do you mean?"

"There was something funny at the dormitory—at Burwood Hall—tonight. Everyone was downstairs, behind closed doors. What was it?"

"Everyone?" Denny said slowly. He was stalling. Upon reflection, he was not surprised that Paula had wind of something unusual happening. Eddie King, the sports editor of the *Daily Cowboy Times*, was fond of dropping around Burwood Hall during the evening in the middle of the week, seeking tidbits of information for his column. More often than not, Eddie arrived before the last of the players were finished with their evening meal. The cafeteria was open. He sometimes went down to the cafeteria to visit with the players there. Eddie would have noticed the closed door. He might have noticed, too, that some familiar faces—those belonging to the offensive crew —were missing from the group playing cards and watching television in the sitting room.

"Well, no, not everyone, but —"

"See," Denny exclaimed gleefully, "you're imagining things."

There was a pause. "Eddie said —"

Denny interrupted her. "Eddie said, Eddie said. I

can't wait to read his story in the morning. The mystery will intrigue me the whole night through."

She sighed. "There's no story. He —"

Denny didn't hear the rest of her sentence. He was relieved that Eddie King, for all his suspicions, did not have enough to publish a story telling the world that the Sutton State Cowboys were working on something special behind closed doors.

"Say," he said suddenly, as if Paula had never mentioned the football team, "if I live through Saturday afternoon, let's go to Marty's for dinner. Okay?"

Again there was a pause. Paula said, "Something *is* going on."

"I'll pick you up at the Tri Delt house at seven o'clock—that is, if I can walk. Okay?"

Paula sighed. "Sure."

Denny went to his room, and until he turned out the light and went to bed, he pored over the Cowboys' playbook, still a strange document for a quarterback whose usual duty was running another team's plays.

Boogie snapped off the tape recorder and left the room. Denny remained in bed for a couple of minutes more, staring at the wall, enjoying the protection of the bedclothes from the world outside. Then he threw back the covers and rolled over into a sitting position on the side of the bed. He reached over to the tape recorder and turned it back on. "Hut . . . hut-hut."

He glanced at the playbook, still open on the desk. Maybe it was the playbook that put the frightening question in Denny's brain: What if it doesn't work? Denny was unsure of the Cowboys' plays. He had no practice experience, much less game experience, with the Cowboys' offense. He was on firmer ground directing the Gordon Tech offense than the Cowboys' offense. After all, he had spent a full week running the Engineers' plays. He had never, however, directed a team in the Cowboys' plays.

"Well," he said to himself, rubbing the sleep out of his eyes, "We've got today"—he stopped and thought, This is Wednesday, isn't it?—"and we've got tomorrow."

He got out of bed and stretched his arms above his head. As he walked to the showers the tape recorder was broadcasting, "Quick-six: hut-hut . . . hut-hut . . . hut-hut."

10

Outside the world of football, away from Burwood Hall, off the practice field, out of the dressing room, Denny Westbrook found himself suddenly a celebrity —in more ways than one.

Walking across the campus in the warm morning sunshine of the West Texas autumn, Denny was oblivious to those around him. His mind was still on the telephone conversation with Wally Polk just a few minutes before, when Denny was leaving the dormitory. Two parts of Denny's plan remained to be set up, and the telephone conversation with the coach had confirmed that the wheels were in motion.

"Edmund Albright will do it," Wally Polk told Denny. "Drop by his office early this afternoon, and iron out the details."

"Edmund Albright," Denny repeated. Denny did not know him. He never had heard the name. But Edmund Albright was the man he needed. Albright, was the head of the television drama department. "And John Ellerton?" Denny asked.

"He's agreeable too. No problem at all. He just wanted to know who's paying for it." Wally Polk's voice conveyed clearly his dislike of the intrusion of such trivia when a football game was at stake. "I told him who's paying for it."

Denny grinned at the telephone. He knew about John Ellerton, the chief of the photography section of the journalism department. Paula complained about him incessantly. He always wanted to know in advance who was picking up the tab. "I'll see Ellerton this afternoon, too," Denny said.

"Right," Polk said.

Now crossing the campus, Denny saw the evidence of his newfound celebrity before he recognized it for what it was: People were looking at him, pointing at him, staring. On the sprawling Sutton State campus, with a student body more than 30,000 strong, few students had the sort of fame that made them recognizable to everyone. Louie St. Pierre had it. Everyone on the Sutton State campus knew the quarterback by sight. A few other football players had it—Mike O'Brien, Tim Van Buren, even Earthquake Morrison, who was too large to miss in any crowd. A few basketball players had it, and so did the leading campus politicians. And yes, Paula Bradford, editor of the *Daily Cowboy Times*, was well known on campus. But Denny Westbrook? Who was he?

"That's him," somebody said, as Denny passed a small group in front of the library.

"Me?" Denny asked himself. Then with a shrug and a grin, he said, "Yeah, me."

Denny veered to the south of the library and walked into the side door of the student-union building. He found what he was looking for inside the door: the rack holding Wednesday's edition of the *Daily Cowboy Times*. He picked a copy out of the box. And there, on page one, three columns wide, was his own face staring back at him. The headline over the picture read: *Denny Who?* Denny could not help grinning. Paula Bradford might be Denny's girl friend, but she was, first of all, the editor of the *Daily Cowboy Times*. Denny Westbrook got the same treatment as everyone else.

The headline on the story beneath the picture read:

COWBOYS TO FACE ALLERTON
WITH UNTRIED SUB AT QB

Denny folded the paper, stuffed it into his notebook, and walked back out of the student-union building into the bright sunshine.

Faces that Denny never had seen before gave him smiles. People he did not know said, "Hi ya, Denny." Someone called out, "Good luck, Denny."

In his sports medicine class, Dr. Howard Bridges grinned at Denny and asked, "Are you *the* Denny Westbrook?" The class, mostly athletes who knew Denny from the football team and from phys ed classes, roared with laughter.

"Until Saturday," Denny quipped, and the class roared again.

At noon, heading back to Burwood Hall for lunch, Jerry Burton intercepted Denny in front of the ag building. Jerry was carrying a tape recorder with a portable microphone. "Got a minute?" he asked.

"Sure."

"For an interview?"

Denny looked at the microphone. "I guess so," he said. He could hardly refuse after Jerry had spent almost thirty minutes listening to the chant of "hut . . . hut . . . hut" and then produced the copies of the tape for the team members. "Sure, yeah," Denny said.

Jerry led the way to the edge of the porch of the ag building and settled on the railing. "This will do," he said.

Below them, students heading back to their dormitories for lunch glanced up. Denny heard one of them say, "That's Westbrook."

Jerry smiled at him. "Suddenly you're famous."

"Yeah," Denny said. He admitted to himself that he was enjoying it.

Jerry punched a button on the tape recorder, and the machine began a soft whirring.

"This is Jerry Burton with Denny Westbrook on the campus. Denny has been designated the quarterback for the Cowboys against the Allerton Lions on Saturday." Jerry spoke into the microphone without looking at Denny. Denny was struck by Jerry's voice, deeper than his normal conversational tone. He also clipped the words in a strange way. "Denny, are you aware of the pressure building up on Coach Polk in the wake of his decision to play you at quarterback against Allerton?"

Denny blinked in surprise. "No, I'm not," he said.

"Let me fill you in," Jerry said in his staccato style. "There's been a lot of criticism of Coach Polk's decision to play you at quarterback. Austin Henderson, the president of the Sutton Club, said in Houston this morning that Coach Polk had taken leave of his senses. Those were Austin Henderson's words. And the president of the Sutton State Alumni Association, Leroy Campbell, said in Fort Worth that he is complaining to the president of the university about what he called Coach Polk's stubborn refusal to reconsider the suspension of Louie St. Pierre in light of subsequent events."

"Uh-huh," Denny said absently. "I'm afraid that I don't know anything about it."

"The heat is building up," Jerry announced into the microphone. "And while we all know this is very difficult for you, I'd like to ask what you think about it."

Denny glared at Jerry. This question was not what Denny had in mind when he agreed to an interview. Obviously, he thought, there is more to being a celebrity than having strangers smile and wave at you and wish you good luck. Jerry returned Denny's stare in a bland, unexpressive way, apparently unaware of the extent of Denny's sudden discomfort.

"I don't think anything about it at all," Denny said finally. "Coach Polk is the coach of the team. Not Mr. Henderson. And not Mr. Campbell. And Coach Polk said that I am going to be the quarterback on Saturday, and that is what I will do—be the quarterback, to the best of my ability."

For a frightening second, Denny was sure that Jerry was going to ask about the tapes—"hut . . . hut . . . hut"—and reveal to his listeners that the unknown quarterback had some surprises up his sleeve for the Allerton Lions.

But Jerry said only, "Good luck to you, Denny." And then, after a pause, he added, "This is Jerry Burton reporting from on campus with Denny Westbrook, the surprise quarterback choice of the Cowboys against the Allerton Lions." Jerry clicked off the tape recorder.

Denny concluded that Abner Shell knew what he was talking about when he said Jerry Burton could be counted on for confidentiality.

"Thanks," Jerry said. "That was a good answer."

Denny frowned at him. "That was a bad question," he said. "You could've let me know what was coming."

106

"I'm sorry. I assumed that you did know. It was in all the papers this morning—the *Daily Cowboy Times*, the Dallas paper, the Houston paper, El Paso —all of 'em. And it was on all the radio sportscasts."

"I haven't had a lot of time for reading the papers or listening to the radio lately," Denny said coldly.

Jerry grimaced. "I'm sorry, really. I didn't know." He paused. "Anyway, that was a good answer you gave."

By the time Denny reached Burwood Hall for lunch, the old question of the early-morning hours— what if?—was ricocheting through his brain again. This time other voices besides Denny's were asking the question. There was the voice of Austin Henderson and the voice of Leroy Campbell. Was there also the voice of Wally Polk?

What if it doesn't work?

In the cafeteria at Burwood Hall, the question "what if?" seemed stamped on the faces of all the football players. Was it Denny's imagination? He thought a conversation came to a sudden halt in midsentence when he stepped into line with his tray. He thought another conversation stopped, again in midsentence, when he put his tray on a table and sat down to eat. To Denny, everyone seemed to be silent all of a sudden.

The gimmicks had worn off, Denny knew. The secret drill last night, with the tables pushed back against the wall, had caught everyone's fancy—for the moment. The new plays, the big surprises, had sparked the imagination of them all—for the moment. The horror of the afternoon's practice session was forgotten. The scary idea of playing the Allerton Lions with an undersized fourth-string quarterback short on skills was shoved into the background. An aura of intrigue and of hope prevailed. The new game was, in a way, fun and fascinating. But the morning had come for the other players, Denny knew, the same as it had come for him. Welcome back to the world of reality! Denny had huddled in the bedclothes with a feeling of fright, of terrible uncertainty. How many of the other players had felt the same?

Denny wolfed down the lunch with hardly a word and went to his room. Alone, he stared at himself in the mirror for a full minute. His face looked like the one on the front page of the *Daily Cowboy Times*. Denny who? Denny took a deep breath. His plan might not look as good today as it had last night or the night before when he mapped it out on paper at the study table. But it was all he had, and there was more to be done.

Edmund Albright looked up from his desk when Denny walked into the office. Albright was a heavy man with thick features—full lips, a wide nose, broad cheekbones—and long, wavy black hair. The office was unlike anything Denny had seen at Sutton State.

108

Most of the buildings on the campus were stone or brick in a sort of Mexican style—"Alamo Gothic," the students called it—and the offices in the buildings matched the dullness of the outside. But Albright's office was all chromium and glass and bright colors. Huge color portraits of television stars adorned the walls.

"All set?" Denny asked. He smiled brightly. He tried to sound upbeat. He tried to keep the question of what if from dancing through his mind and showing on his face, but his effort was falling short of success. At this very moment, he knew, Wally Polk might well be asking himself the same question. And he might be listening to all the others who were asking it: Austin Henderson, Leroy Campbell, the players, the newspaper and television reporters. Wally Polk might be changing his mind at this very instant.

"It's a very unusual request," Albright said. "Videotaping and closed-circuit transmission are not easy things to set up. Nor are they inexpensive."

"I know," Denny said. He was slightly puzzled. Wally Polk had told him that Edmund Albright was prepared to cooperate. But now Albright seemed to be uncertain.

"But, yes," Albright said, "we will be set to go along with you."

Denny grinned. "Great!" he said. "It'll be a big help." Then he added, "We're going to need all the help we can get."

"I'm not much of a football fan," Albright said. He waved a hand slightly, indicating that he did not intend to become a football fan. "But Coach Polk said it was some kind of emergency."

"Yes," Denny said. "Yes, some kind of emergency."

"A question occurred to me this morning after I spoke with Coach Polk," Albright said. "You're talking about having a sideline television monitor for instant replays."

"Yes."

"Well, what if it rains?"

"Rains?" Denny said. The question startled him. "It hasn't rained out here in a hundred years. But even if it does. . . ."

"Is it imperative that the monitor be located on the sideline, I mean, outdoors?"

"Yes, imperative."

Denny's plan called for a camera crew in the press box to videotape the entire game. When the Cowboys were on the defense and Denny was on the bench, he could call up the last sequence of his plays and see how they looked from on high.

All teams had some system for telling the coaches and players on the field what the game looked like from above. For most, the scheme involved an assistant coach in the press box with a telephone connection to the bench. But Denny wanted more than verbal advice. He wanted to see the picture for himself. The overview of what went wrong—or, he cor-

110

rected himself, what went right—would be valuable information each time he took the field for another series of downs. If the Allerton defense offered a single chink in the armor, Denny wanted to know it right away. A defensive back drifting too far to one side, a linebacker committing himself too quickly, an interior lineman slow on the takeoff, all these errors spelled opportunity. And this was no game for the Sutton State Cowboys to be passing up a single opportunity, no matter how small.

"If it's important," Albright said, "we'll work something out. We'll be there and ready."

"That's great." Denny grinned, and with a wave of his hand he walked out the door.

A block away, in the journalism building, Denny went up a flight of stairs, down a corridor, and then back down another flight of stairs. The circuitous route was necessary to avoid the *Daily Cowboy Times* editorial offices. He did not want to risk encountering Paula. There would be questions, explanations, more questions. When he reached the photography department, he peeped in briefly, making sure Paula was not there on one of her routine visits making assignments for pictures. She was nowhere in sight, and Denny walked in.

John Ellerton, tall and thin with straight gray hair and wire-rim glasses, was scanning negatives at a stand-up light table. He looked up. "You're Westbrook?"

"Right," Denny said. "Coach Polk called you, didn't he?"

"Yes. He did not say exactly what he wanted us to do—said that you would explain—but he made it clear that we were to do it." Ellerton seemed less than pleased at finding himself the recipient of instructions delivered in Wally Polk's abrupt style. Then he said, "The athletic department is paying for it, so we are yours."

Denny glanced back at the door and spoke quickly. Paula might walk in at any minute. "I need two photographers with Polaroid cameras—cameras that will make the largest possible prints—and lots of film, shooting pictures from the roof of the press box, pictures of every single play that we run against Allerton."

"Every play?"

"Every play—on offense," Denny said.

Ellerton nodded.

"And I need four runners to deliver the pictures right away to me on the sideline during the game."

Ellerton looked at Denny quizzically. "You building a scrapbook?"

Denny grinned. "When I come off the field after a series of downs, I need to see the pictures of the plays that we've just run, to see what the defense was doing. I need as many pictures as I can get, and I need them in hand on the sideline right away."

"Uh-huh," Ellerton said. "I see. Okay. No problem."

Leaving, Denny again skirted around the *Daily Cowboy Times* editorial offices and came out of the journalism building into the bright sunlight of the early afternoon. He paused a moment on the sidewalk. There were few students around. The one o'clock classes were half done. He stretched his arms and heaved a great sigh.

"Everything is set," he said aloud.

But Denny knew when he spoke that he was kidding himself.

11

First there was the flurry about Louie St. Pierre coming back, his suspension lifted.

"Let me tell you, Coach Polk will take him back. He's got to. He's got no choice."

The speaker was Ernie Watson, the Cowboys' student manager. He was straddling a straight chair, his arms crossed on top of the chair's back. The players around him in the sitting room in Burwood Hall perked up their ears—Denny, Lamar Henry, Richie Carson, Tim Van Buren, Earthquake Morrison, Sandy Ruzzo. They all knew that Ernie Watson heard too much while performing his chores with the equipment during the off-hours in the dressing room. They also knew that Ernie talked too much about what he heard.

The players were lounging through the half hour between dinner and the convening of the offensive unit in the basement cafeteria for the second round of secret work. Other players were in their rooms, passing the time writing letters or catching up on their studies. A player occasionally passed the double doors of the sitting room as he headed for the pay telephone on the wall. It was a quiet time in Burwood Hall.

Denny glanced up when Ernie spoke. The sports section of a Dallas newspaper was lying open on the coffee table in front of the sofa where Denny was seated. Denny had read the paper. The sports page told the same story that Ernie was relating: Wally Polk will have to take Louie St. Pierre back. Wally Polk could not afford the risk of doing otherwise. The sportswriter had spelled out the scenario in cold logic.

Louie was healthy, able, and available. The only barrier was some ridiculous disciplinary action taken when the Cowboys thought they had two backup quarterbacks waiting in the wings. Now the backup quarterbacks, both of them, were out. One had an ailing ankle that refused to mend. The other had a shoulder separation suffered in a freak accident. Next in line was an unknown, Denny Westbrook. He was a career redshirt who never had seen the first moment of action in a varsity game. If there ever had been any hope that the unknown Denny Westbrook was a sleeping giant, a quarterback genius waiting quietly in the shadows, it all had vanished in the first practice session: a classic display of fumbles, misthrown passes, off-balance hand-offs.

Now there were grumbles among the Cowboy players—unnamed in the article—and loud howls from powerful alumni and fans all across the state. So, concluded the sportswriter, Wally Polk was bound to bow to the facts of life. He would reconsider Louie St. Pierre's suspension. He would accept Louie's promise never to stray again. And he would save the Cowboys from the humiliation and defeat certain to be theirs if they faced the Allerton Lions without a "real quarterback" at the helm. All the answers seemed so simple in print.

"I read the paper," Denny said to Ernie. Denny sighed. The open discussion of his shortcomings did not bother him. Denny had no illusions about his playing abilities as a quarterback. But he was rapidly growing weary of the speculation—in the press, by Ernie Watson, anybody anywhere. "It's all in the papers," he said.

"Yeah, but you didn't hear what I heard."

Everybody, Denny included, leaned forward.

Ernie cast a quick glance at the double doors opening from the sitting room into the corridor. From anyone else, the gesture would have been an outlandish parody of a furtive glance. From Ernie Watson, it was standard procedure before the relating of some valued tidbit of information.

"You know who Austin Henderson is?"

Everyone looked at Lamar Henry. Lamar smiled.

"Lamar knows who he is," Earthquake Morrison said with a wide grin.

The story of the wealthy Houston oilman's pursuit

116

of Lamar Henry for his alma mater's football team was legend in the football circles of Sutton State. And now Lamar worked in the summers for Henderson's oil firm in Houston as a business administration trainee.

"I don't know who he is," Denny said with a straight face. He couldn't resist the remark, especially after reading in the paper that Austin Henderson considered Denny Westbrook a disaster looking for a place to happen.

Ernie shot a puzzled glance at Denny. Everyone at Sutton State knew the name of Austin Henderson. When everybody roared with laughter, Ernie said, "Oh."

Then he recovered his balance. "Henderson called Coach Polk this afternoon. The door to the office was open. I couldn't help hearing."

"Yeah, sure," Earthquake said.

Ernie looked offended. "Look, you want to hear this or not?"

Denny asked, "Shall I excuse myself?"

Earthquake got to his feet in mock anger. "If Denny leaves, I leave," he boomed.

Denny grinned at the huge lineman.

"Seriously, you guys," Ernie pleaded.

Denny glanced around the room. The players were all friends of his. But nobody was fooling anybody about the Cowboys' quarterback problem. For four years they all, Denny included, had known Denny's limitations as a quarterback, and now they all, Denny included, knew they were in a jam.

"Please do continue," Denny said finally in a courtly manner. "After all, this relates to whether or not I get killed on Saturday. As you can understand, I am interested." He waved a hand, signaling Ernie to resume.

Earthquake sat back down, grinning broadly, obviously pleased with himself for upsetting Ernie.

Ernie gave the double doors another quick glance. "Well, all I heard was one side of the conversation, you understand," he said. "I couldn't hear what Henderson was saying on his end of the line."

"Ernie, I don't know about you," Earthquake said.

"He's not into bugging yet," Denny said.

"How come you're not into bugging?" Earthquake asked.

Ernie ignored them. The other players were waiting for what he had to tell. Denny was too, and even Earthquake, still grinning, was watching Ernie and ready to listen.

"I gather that Louie had called Henderson," Ernie said.

"Louie called Henderson!" Lamar Henry blurted.

Denny agreed with Lamar's disbelief. Even Louie St. Pierre would not try anything so foolish as going over Wally Polk's head.

"Yeah," Ernie said, "because Coach Polk kept

118

saying, 'I don't care what he told you. I've made my decision, and it sticks.' "

The room was silent a moment.

"More likely, Henderson called Louie," Lamar said. He was the resident expert on Austin Henderson. "That's sort of Henderson's style."

"And Louie would be dumb enough to talk to him," Richie Carson chimed in.

"Jeez," Earthquake muttered. "Coach Polk will have the head of everybody in sight."

"Well, anyway," Ernie continued, "I guess that Louie promised that he never would break the rules again, or Henderson was making the promise for him, because then Coach Polk said, 'We run this team on performances, not promises.' Then there was a minute of silence while Henderson was talking, and then Coach Polk said, 'I am fully aware that the game is important'—those were his exact words—'but some things are more important than this game.' Then he hung up. I mean, just hung up, without another word."

Denny glanced down at the sports page on the coffee table in front of him. His mind went back to the quotation attributed to Austin Henderson: "Usually coaches win if they can; if they can't, they build character. Wally Polk seems to have got himself all mixed up on this question." Denny wondered if Wally Polk had seen the quotation. Probably so, and he was in no mood to take Austin Henderson's advice. But still,

Denny knew, winning and losing mattered—to Wally Polk, to the players, and yes, to Austin Henderson.

"Sounds pretty hot," Lamar said.

"It was."

Nobody said anything for a moment.

Then Tim Van Buren, speaking softly, said, "Henderson swings a lot of weight with this football team. You know, recruiting help and all that. And he does, you know, represent the fans. He's president of the Sutton Club."

Denny shrugged. "It seems to me that Coach Polk told Henderson, as politely as possible, to go jump in a lake."

There was some nodding of heads around the room.

Denny was aware, not without some amazement, of the strange detachment he felt. Here he was, sitting in on a discussion of the pressures on the coach to play somebody, anybody, at quarterback other than himself. Denny smiled to himself. Four years on the redshirt team had prepared him perfectly for this moment. He knew that if some development kept him on the bench in the Allerton game, he had lost nothing. He never had existed, really, as a first-string quarterback. He was not giving up anything—anything at all. And if he did play the game, he needed only to be one small notch above a total disaster to surprise everyone. Strangely, he felt himself beyond the furor, outside the pressure. He told himself these things time and again, in order to keep one thought far, far in the back of his mind: He wanted to play the game.

Ernie was not finished. "But you don't know what happened later, right after practice this afternoon." Ernie always enjoyed feeding listeners his tasty items slowly, tantalizingly.

"Oh?" Earthquake said. "There's more?"

"Louie and Mike O'Brien and Dutch Hauser went into Coach Polk's office." Ernie paused and let the impact of his latest news bulletin sink in on his audience. "Coach Polk sent Mike and Dutch right back out, but he kept Louie in there, and he called in Bucky Summers."

Denny thought, No wonder Ernie has been keeping an eye on the doors to the corridor. Mike or Dutch, or even Louie, might appear at any moment.

Denny's mind went back to a particular scene—meaningless at the time—just as today's practice was coming to an end. Denny was finishing his wind sprints and turning to head for the dressing room. Louie, who had spent the session jogging around the perimeter of the field, was walking away with Mike and Dutch. They were talking. There was nothing odd about it. The three were good friends of long standing. Bucky Summers, off to the side, was breaking away from a brief interview with one of the television crews that had been filming parts of the practice session. Bucky joined Louie and Mike and Dutch for the walk to the dressing room. They were talking as they went on their way.

"Bucky Summers," Denny said under his breath, and he remembered what Wally Polk had told him: The vote was six to one.

"Yeah," Ernie said, "and the three of them were in there with the door closed for thirty minutes."

"After practice?" Richie Carson asked. "After Coach Polk had talked with Austin Henderson?"

"Yeah."

"Wow! I'll bet Coach Polk burned Louie a tattoo," Richie said.

"I wonder," Tim Van Buren said thoughtfully.

"I couldn't hear a thing through the door," Ernie said.

"Ernie, you're not worth a hoot when we need you," Earthquake said.

Denny grinned at Earthquake. Then his eyes moved around the room. He saw Lamar Henry, Earthquake Morrison, Richie Carson, Tim Van Buren, the others. None of them were the players who were disgruntled by Wally Polk's decision to put the quarterbacking assignment in Denny Westbrook's hands. They were worried perhaps, but not disgruntled. Uncertain perhaps, but still supportive of Denny. Mike O'Brien was the one who had complained about Denny from the start. Dutch Hauser was the one who doubted Denny's ability even to handle the snaps from

122

center. So the two of them, with Louie, had gone to the coach to plead with him to save them from the disaster of Denny Westbrook as quarterback.

Denny was not surprised. Today's practice had been no better than yesterday's. Mike O'Brien had kept his mouth shut on the field. He apparently wanted no more of Denny's threats to expel him from the huddle. But the disgust showed on his face. And Dutch, sending his center snaps into unfamiliar hands, had left no doubt that he considered the quarterback behind him to be inept, unworthy, and dangerous.

Denny frowned. He refused to let the opinions of Mike O'Brien and Dutch Hauser—and undoubtedly some of the other players—bother him. There was nothing he could do about their concern anyway. But for another reason the episode was cause for worry. Wally Polk was catching heat. He was catching heat from the press, the alumni, the fans. And now, it seemed, he was catching heat from his own players.

Denny pulled himself away from his thoughts when the front door opened and he heard the unmistakable tones of Wally Polk's husky voice in the corridor.

Hank Wilson stuck his head into the sitting room. "Okay, let's go," he said.

Denny spotted Wally Polk walking past the door. He got up and took off after the coach. He caught him in the corridor leading to the basement stairs. "Am I still it?" he asked.

Polk, startled, turned and gazed at Denny. His

expression seemed to say: You know something that you're not supposed to know. Denny's heart was in his throat.

"You're it," Polk said flatly, and led the way down the stairs.

12

But only moments later Denny got the first indication that the final flutter in the storm over Louie St. Pierre's punishment was yet to come.

Stepping out of the doorway at the foot of the stairs and walking into the basement, Denny caught Louie's eye. The tall, lanky quarterback was standing against a wall, leaning easily, with his arms folded over his chest. In the second that their eyes met, Louie nodded. The small smile that always seemed to say, "Who cares?" was missing from Louie's face. Louie was staring soberly at Denny, almost as if he had been waiting and watching for him.

Denny returned the nod of greeting. Then, frowning, he walked toward the front of the room. He was puzzled. Always before, in the three years they had known each other, Louie had seemed to be looking through, rather than at, Denny. This time he was acting differently. Denny could not help wondering why.

Denny reran the words of Ernie Watson's story in

his mind. He pondered the gaps in it. What had happened behind the closed doors? What had been said? Did Wally Polk simply listen and then growl No, ending the matter? Or did he explain, patiently and in detail, the reasons for his firm stand?

What had Louie St. Pierre said? And Bucky Summers? Dutch Hauser? And, in the end, had they agreed with—or at least accepted—the coach's decision?

Wally Polk rapped his knuckles on a stack of trays at the head of the steam table. The noise ended the questions in Denny's mind. He turned and looked at the coach. The room fell silent.

"There's been some speculation," Polk said. "You've heard the rumors and you've read the newspaper stories and you've heard the reporters on the radio and on television."

Denny stared at the floor.

"But I am here to tell you that Denny Westbrook will be our quarterback on Saturday against Allerton." He paused. "Any questions?"

The room was silent. Nobody even shuffled a foot on the tile floor.

"For better or for worse," Denny said to himself.

"All right then," Polk said, "let's get to work."

Denny looked up and glanced around the room. Louie St. Pierre had left.

From the start the drill was sluggish. With the now-familiar tape recording barking the signals,

126

Denny and the others went through the motions—the backfield men rehearsing the new plays, the linemen adjusting themselves to the cadence they would be hearing on Saturday. But nothing seemed to work. Dutch Hauser's snaps from center, instead of being quick and crisp, were casual, lackadaisical. Mark Madison fumbled. The linemen were ragged in their charge. Mike O'Brien's anger showed at every turn. The other players—Richie Carson, even Tim Van Buren—had lost the enthusiasm that seemed so infectious only one night earlier. Denny could see the difference in their eyes. He could mark it in their movements. The intrigue of the secret workout, the excitement of the conspiracy, the gimmick of the tape-recorded snap signals, the possibilities of the new strategies, even the camaraderie that had come with knowing they would be playing without an experienced and able quarterback were evaporating now.

Denny tried, and at first Earthquake helped, to keep the chatter going, to lift the players back to the enthusiasm and determination of the first night. The coaches too barked, cajoled, and at one point tried to joke the players out of their flat, listless performance. Finally Earthquake, and then Denny, gave up the charade, and in the end the coaches themselves seemed to let the drill coast to a finish.

Denny trooped upstairs with the silent crowd of players. He told himself that he had to believe the plan would work, even if nobody else did. He had to believe the Cowboys could win with Denny West-brook at quarterback. Then the others would believe. They would have to believe.

Denny came out at the head of the staircase and immediately saw Louie St. Pierre. In that instant, Denny had the feeling that Louie had been waiting for him. Strangely, he was not surprised.

Louie approached. "Got a minute?" he asked softly.

"Huh?"

"A minute?"

The other players, taking no notice, were streaming by, heading for the sitting room or up another flight of stairs to their own rooms.

"Oh, sure," Denny said.

Louie led the way to the front door. Denny followed. Louie opened the door and stepped out onto the porch. Denny went with him.

On the porch they were alone. The autumn evening was cool, comfortably so. Neither of them sat. They stood facing each other. Louie, nearly a foot taller, towered over Denny. Denny looked up. In the darkness, he could not see Louie's face well. But he could tell that the mocking half smile was still missing from it.

"How'd it go?" Louie asked.

Denny did not speak for a moment. He wondered, Is this really Louie St. Pierre? Then he said, "Not very well."

Louie answered with, "Uh-huh."

There was a pause.

"He's going to stick by his guns," Louie said.

"Yes."

"I really cooked myself this time."

Denny said nothing. He squinted into the shadows, trying to see Louie's face clearly. He couldn't. Perhaps the face would have given some clue as to what was on Louie's mind. Did Louie see his all-America rating, so certain a week ago, going down the drain? Did he see his prospects of a professional football career, so bright a week ago, flickering out? Or did he see the Cowboys floundering without their quarterback, taking a smashing defeat, and plummeting in the national rankings, all because of his misbehavior? Denny could not tell.

"Really cooked it," Louie said. "I thought he would back down. I really thought he would. But he's not going to."

"Yes," Denny said. Then he added quickly, "I mean, I thought he might back down at first myself. At first. But now . . . no, he's not going to back down. He's made his decision."

There was a moment of silence. Louie shifted his weight uneasily from one foot to the other. Denny reflected that this conversation was, to the best of his memory—no, for certain—the first he ever had had with Louie St. Pierre. The two of them—the star quarterback, surefire all-America, and the fourth-stringer—talking, one on one. Louis St. Pierre was a star. He always had been. He always would be. His friends were stars. There was no time for anyone else. What did the others matter anyway?

Denny wondered, Why now? There had to be a reason. Something was coming. Denny was sure of it. He remembered the glance—*at* him, not *through* him —and the nod from Louie in the basement. Louie had something on his mind.

Denny took a deep breath. He dreaded what was coming, no matter what it might be. From the moment of Wally Polk's telephone call on Monday night, he had taken comfort in the absence of Louie St. Pierre from his world. He had been relieved he was not stepping in for a friend who had been suspended. Louie was not a friend. There was solace in the fact that Louie and his remarks were out of earshot. The anger of Mike O'Brien, the dull stares of Dutch Hauser, the concerned expressions of the others were enough. Denny did not need mocking grins or cutting remarks from Louie St. Pierre.

"I want to ask you a favor," Louie said.

"A favor?" So that was it. Louie wanted Denny to join the pleading of the case. He wanted Denny to go to Wally Polk and urge a lifting of the suspension. Wally Polk could not refuse. "What favor?" Denny asked.

"I want to be on the sideline with the team on Saturday."

130

Denny was ready to refuse to plead with Polk for Louie's reinstatement. The matter was simply none of his business. But he was not prepared for what Louie had actually said.

"That's . . ."

"He says that I'm suspended, and that means no practice, and it means no dressing out for the game."

"Oh," Denny said. "I see."

"I could be a help to you," Louie said. Then he added, "I want to be there." He paused. "If you were to ask. . . ." The words trailed off.

Denny wished he could see Louie's face. This voice sounded like a different Louie St. Pierre, one that nobody knew. Maybe Wally Polk really—*really*—knew what he was doing when he expelled Louie from the team for a week. The discipline might cost the Cowboys a victory. But it might be the making of a great quarterback. However, Denny could not see Louie's face. The shadows were too deep.

The answers to the request were whirling through Denny's brain. They all were negative, all of them. What help would Louie be on the sideline? None. His advice could not make Denny execute the plays better. He did not know the game plan better than Denny, if he knew it at all. No, he would be no help. So why plead for him?

On the other hand, there were plenty of reasons why he shouldn't plead for him. The players along the sideline, seeing Louie, would be waiting for a nod

131

from the coach sending him into the game. No matter that things are going badly, they would think. Louie can save the day. But there was going to be no Louie St. Pierre on the field against Allerton. Better that the players knew it and realized the fact beyond a doubt. The crowd, seeing Louie on the sideline, might set up a roar for him. And Denny, struggling on the field, would run every play under the shadow of the great Louie St. Pierre. No, the eyes of the crowd and the television audience were enough. The eyes of Louie St. Pierre watching from the sideline were two eyes too many.

For an instant, Denny was tempted to answer No. The one word was more than Louie St. Pierre had spoken to him in three years. He considered trying to explain what he saw as Wally Polk's reasoning in the decision. But surely Louie already understood.

"I think this is something that Coach Polk will have to decide," Denny said finally.

Louie shifted his weight again. "Okay," he said. He made no move to return to the house.

Denny waited.

"Well," Louie said finally, "good luck."

Denny saw Louie's right hand extended. He took it. They shook. "Thanks," Denny said. "I'll need it."

13

Then there was the controversy over the health of John Porter's right ankle.

"You mean you haven't heard?" Paula asked.

It was Thursday noon. She and Denny were seated in a booth in the student-union cafeteria. They were having a lunch of cheeseburgers and Cokes. Denny had called her at the last minute to meet him for lunch. He had decided·to skip lunch at Burwood Hall. He did not want to see Mike O'Brien's face, the teeth clenched. He did not want to look at Dutch Hauser's expressionless face. He did not want to see Louie St. Pierre, with or without the mocking half grin. He did not want to hear the latest from Ernie Watson. He did not want to ask himself again, What if it doesn't work? The players, all of them, reminded him of the question.

Denny had been eating quietly, his mind occupied with totaling up a set of figures: In another five hours his last heavy drill as a first-string quarterback would be over; in another thirty hours the final signal-calling

133

drill of Friday would have been run; in thirty-six hours the campus pep rally, where he would have to step forward as the quarterback, would be over; and in—how many?—fifty-four hours the game would be finished. Fifty-four hours left till the end of the crazy week.

"What?" Denny asked. "I'm afraid I wasn't listening."

"You didn't know that they're taking John Porter to the doctor again? He's there now. They took him late this morning. They want the doctor to take one last look at his ankle."

Denny gulped down the bite of hamburger. He was hearing Paula now. "Where did you hear that?"

"Eddie King. He's gone with them."

"Do they think John will be able to play?" Denny recalled the picture of John, with his crutches, leaning against the wall during the previous night's drill in the basement cafeteria. Then he answered his own question. "He's in no shape to play," he said.

"According to Eddie, the theory is that he might be able to stand up there and throw passes if he got good protection."

"Ummm."

"Seems that he walked on the ankle a bit this morning and said it wasn't too painful."

"I didn't see him walking on it."

"It's just the story that Eddie got. Maybe with some pain-killer shots. . . ."

134

"Coach Polk would never do that," Denny said.

"Well, I don't know," Paula said with a shrug. "But I guess we'll have the verdict in a little while."

Denny said nothing. If the doctor was persuaded that John Porter could play without danger of serious injury, Denny Westbrook was on his way back to the bench. He would watch the game from the sideline, as always, with his helmet in his hand. For a moment, Denny felt a sense of relief. He caught himself hoping that John Porter, through some sort of miracle, would be able to walk out of the doctor's office without the crutches, smiling and ready to play. With one word from the doctor, the burden would be off Denny's back. He would no longer be the quarterback. He would no longer face the unhappy fate of being the instrument of doom for his teammates. He would no longer be destined to fail disastrously before the stunned eyes of 60,000 fans in the Cowboys' stadium and millions more watching on television. For Denny, the craziest week in his life would have ended, blessedly, ahead of schedule.

No longer would he have to ask himself, What if it doesn't work? No more would Mike O'Brien look angry. No longer would Denny see the hopelessness stamped on Dutch Hauser's face. Gone would be the expressions of concern on the faces of his friends—Tim, Boogie, the others. No more would Earthquake Morrison have to deliver play-acting reassurances.

Bucky Summers would have a quarterback for his

offense. Wally Polk would have a victory for the record books. The Cowboys would remain high in the national rankings, heading for a postseason bowl game. Austin Henderson would be happy. Everyone would be happy.

But no! Denny remembered the vote had been six to one. Denny wanted to prove Wally Polk right. He wanted to prove the others wrong. Denny had his plan. He wanted to prove that the plan would work. He wanted to show the players—his friends Tim, Earthquake, Boogie and the others, Mike, Dutch, and yes, Louie St. Pierre—that he could win. He wanted to show the world that the Sutton State Cowboys could win with Denny Westbrook at quarterback. His brain rather than his muscle was to face the test. His ingenuity, rather than his skill, was on the line. For all his wobbly passes, awkward hand-offs, and uncertain runs, Denny knew that he could win. He wanted to prove it. He wanted to play.

Paula broke the silence. "Would you be disappointed or relieved?" she asked.

Denny grinned at her. "I think I'll turn out to be better than any of the one-legged quarterbacks around," he said.

The word was buzzing all over Burwood Hall when Denny arrived to drop off his books and check his mail.

136

Richie Carson, coming out of the sitting room, met Denny in the corridor. "You heard?"

"Yeah."

"I mean, have they decided anything? I figured that you would. . . ." Richie let his voice trail off.

"No, I don't know," Denny said.

With the lunch hour ending, groups of players were coming up from the basement cafeteria.

"John was walking without his crutches this morning," Sandy Ruzzo said. "He was limping a little but said it seemed okay to him."

Denny looked at the little field-goal kicker. Sandy was hardly any more of a physical specimen than Denny himself. Yes, Denny thought, Sandy is hoping that John can play. Sandy wants a quarterback in the game who can put touchdowns on the scoreboard. Otherwise, the burden is on Sandy to win the game with field goals from thirty yards out.

"Are they back yet?" Denny asked.

"I haven't seen John."

Ernie Watson breezed by. "No word yet," he announced. If Ernie did not know the final verdict, nobody did. "I'll let you know," he said.

Denny climbed the stairs to his room on the second floor. Boogie Hadley was poring over a textbook at the desk. Beside him the tape recorder was turned on, soft and low: "Hut . . . hut . . . hut-hut."

To Denny, the sound of his own voice barking the

signals sounded a little ridiculous now. The whole plan was going down the tubes. It had been a silly thing anyway.

"Looks like you won't be needing that now," Denny said, gesturing at the tape recorder.

Boogie looked up. Then he glanced at the tape recorder. He said, "Oh, I don't know."

"They've taken John back to the doctor for another look."

"Ah, don't pay any attention to that. It's just politics."

"Politics?"

"Sure. Coach Polk is under all kinds of pressure, see. He fought 'em off on Louie's suspension. He couldn't do anything else. He had to stand his ground. Discipline and all that, you know. So now the heat's on to play John if it's at all possible. So Polk has taken John to the doctor one more time to prove that it's not possible for John to play. That's all. I don't see why everybody is so worked up."

"I heard that he was walking without his crutches this morning."

"Yeah, I saw that. That's why I'm so sure it's just politics. You should have seen him."

"Maybe. . . ."

Boogie turned in the chair and grinned up at Denny. "You're not going to get off the hook that easy, Westbrook. It's like Earthquake said. We're going to make a star out of you on Saturday."

138

Denny did not feel like smiling. He shrugged. "I'll be there," he said.

Denny picked his mail off the desk, stuffed it in his psych spiral notebook, and walked out of the room.

Halfway down the stairs he heard his name being called out in the corridor below.

"Yeah, here," he shouted.

"Phone," came the reply.

"Got it," Denny called out, skipping down the remaining half-dozen steps and walking to the instrument on the wall. The receiver was dangling at the end of its wire. Denny picked it up.

"Hello."

"Denny?" The voice was Wally Polk's.

Denny felt his heart leap. "Yes, sir."

"Before you ask again, let me tell you: You are still it on Saturday."

Denny was silent a moment.

"You there?"

"Yes, sir."

14

Then a funny thing happened.

Suddenly, out of nowhere, the Sutton State campus, and perhaps the whole state of Texas, and maybe the whole world, was swept with what one sportswriter called "Denny fever."

Nobody knew where it began. But outside the team, away from the practice field, out of the locker room and out of Burwood Hall, the epidemic exploded and spread in all directions.

The first symptoms appeared on Thursday afternoon after Wally Polk told the reporters and television crews now jamming the corridors of the field house, "For the last time, yes, Denny Westbrook is our quarterback for the Allerton game."

This time the world believed Wally Polk. The question of lifting Louie St. Pierre's suspension had been fought out and finally settled. The answer was no. The last lingering possibility of John Porter's miracle recovery evaporated in a single word from the doctor: No. At this late date, there was no point in arguing the merits of converting Lamar Henry or Mike O'Brien into a quarterback. The shouting was done, the protests finished, the objections all registered and rejected.

It was a fact: Denny Westbrook, undersized, unskilled, and inexperienced, was the Cowboys' quarterback for the Allerton game.

Among the players, nothing changed. For them, the blush of Denny fever had been brief, and out of sight of the rest of the world. The intrigue of the secret drills in the basement of Burwood Hall created a sense of camaraderie. The new plays gave hope. The startling tactical innovations sparked the imagination. For the moment, the shortcomings of Denny Westbrook as a quarterback did not matter. To the contrary, they helped. The Cowboys were going to win with Denny. The prospect was exciting. Denny fever had been kindled, but it was short-lived, swept aside on the practice field by Denny's ineptitude. For the players, from the angry Mike O'Brien to the joking Earthquake Morrison, whatever there had been of Denny fever had been replaced by reality.

But outside the team, all across the Sutton State campus and the state, Denny fever was building and spreading. At the drills on Thursday afternoon, the crowd on the sidelines of the practice field—students, faculty, other fans—numbered in the hundreds. Ten times more than the usual smattering of onlookers at Cowboys' practice sessions milled around the sidelines and the end zones, jostling each other for a better view. They had turned out to see the marvel of the ages —Denny Who? Unknown, undersized, a shaky passer, an uncertain ball handler, he was—wonder of wonders—the quarterback of the national powerhouse Sutton State Cowboys.

The crowd's curiosity turned to support. The support turned to cheers. Ganged around the end of the field where Denny and his offensive crew were practicing, they sent up deafening roars of approval whenever Denny completed a pass or shot a pitchout back to Mike O'Brien or ran off tackle on a keeper play.

Swarming through the area, they drifted in from the sidelines and up from the goal line until, finally, Wally Polk had to hail Ernie Watson to keep them back. As they retreated behind the chalk lines, they began to chant: "We want Denny. We want Denny."

"See," said Earthquake Morrison. "We're already making a star out of you."

Denny grinned and shook his head in amazement. "Just like Joe Namath—star quality," he quipped.

Around him, the others—Mike, Tim, Dutch, Boogie, all of them—stared at the cheering crowd in puzzlement without saying anything.

At the end of the practice session, Denny walked wearily toward the field house, dangling his helmet in his right hand. The huge shoulder pads seemed to envelop his light frame as he walked. Denny was looking forward to the shower. The crowds were gone now, but the cheers from the sidelines still echoed in his mind. Cheers were a new experience for Denny Westbrook. He had to admit that he had enjoyed them. They were pulling for me, he thought. They really were pulling for me.

Denny went back over the practice session in his mind. While not good by the usual measure, it was the best of the three with Denny at the helm. He was sure of it. He could sense the improvement. He was getting used to his teammates—their speeds, their strengths, their weaknesses. His study of the playbook was paying off. He felt more comfortable each day with the bread-and-butter plays of the Cowboys' attack. With time, he was getting better. But he knew that time was running out.

Suddenly the figure of Mackie Loren, wearing his usual red blazer with a silver spur on the pocket, loomed in front of Denny. Denny smiled at the sports publicity director. If Denny's week was the craziest in football history, Mackie Loren's week was surely running a close second. Dealing with the newspaper reporters and television sportcasters trying to keep track of the Cowboys' quarterback situation was an unnerving job.

"Got a minute for the television boys?" Mackie asked.

The question caught Denny by surprise. Members of the Sutton State Cowboys football team did not hold press conferences, did not grant interviews, and did not appear in front of the television cameras after practice. Nobody ever had written down the rule. Nobody ever even stated it. But everyone understood that Wally Polk did the talking for the team.

"Coach Polk says it's okay," Mackie said. "They just want a comment or two to use on the air in the pregame show on Saturday. You're a new face, you know."

Denny glanced at the television crew, standing off to the side. Apparently Wally Polk was bending all sorts of rules this week. "What'll I say?" Denny asked.

Mackie snorted and took Denny by the arm, leading him toward the television crew. "Westbrook," he said, as they walked, "I've never yet known you to be speechless."

When the bright lights went on in his face, and the announcer stepped alongside him, Denny felt even smaller than his five-foot-seven frame. The announcer, well over six feet tall, hovered over Denny. With a smile, Denny wondered if the television station had intentionally sent the tallest announcer they could find.

"Look into the camera," the announcer said, "and just say in your own words what you think about the Cowboys' prospects against Allerton on Saturday. I'll give you an intro."

Denny nodded.

"Denny, what about the Allerton game?"

144

Denny blinked at the lights and stared at the camera lens. "This is the only chance in my life to play for the Sutton State Cowboys in a game," he said. "You don't think I'm planning on losing, do you?"

The lights went off.

Beyond the cameraman, Denny saw Mackie Loren rolling his eyes.

One of the reporters called out, "Hey, Mackie, did you give him that quote?"

"Believe me," Mackie said, "nobody ever had to give Denny Westbrook a quote."

That night somebody spray painted *Viva Denny* on a wall of the law-school building. And sidewalks all across the campus were carefully stenciled with the same words, *Viva Denny*, in four-inch letters in red paint.

The next morning the *Daily Cowboy Times*' front page carried a photograph of Denny fading back to pass in practice, and the headline over the picture read: *You Don't Think I'm Planning on Losing, Do You?*

A Dallas newspaper carried the same caption over a cartoon showing Denny, even smaller and thinner than in real life, carrying the Sutton State Cowboys team over the goal line.

Denny grinned at the cartoon. The statement was, he knew, a bit pompous. He wondered what Wally Polk thought of it. He wondered what the players thought. Then he shrugged. It expressed his honest feeling, his honest hope, which, who knew, might come true.

At lunch, Earthquake Morrison winked at Denny and said, "I think this thing is getting a little out of hand."

"I don't," Denny said with a grin.

"Jeez," said Mike O'Brien.

Dutch Hauser said nothing.

Boogie Hadley said, "I think Earthquake was off in his timing. He said we'd make a star out of you on Saturday. We've made a star out of you already."

Saturday was one day away. Denny thought of the game coming up with a twinge, but he managed to keep the wide grin on his face.

When Denny arrived at the field house for practice and started walking through the lobby, he heard his name.

"Denny! Denny Westbrook!"

"Huh?" He turned. Mrs. Moody, the athletic department's secretary, waved him into her office.

"You've been getting fan mail," she said. She reached into a basket on her desk and scooped up a stack of telegrams, each still in its small yellow envelope with his name showing through the cellophane window. "You're famous!"

Denny took the stack of a dozen telegrams or more and walked back into the lobby. He was intentionally early for practice, determined to avoid the mob of reporters, and the lobby was empty. He turned and skipped down the stairs to the basement and walked along the corridor until he came to the equipment room.

There, seated on a bench, Denny opened the telegrams one at a time and read them.

The messages put a deepening frown on Denny's face. "We know you can do it." "We're all pulling for you." "We're with you all the way." "Best wishes for a great day." Most of them were signed by people Denny had never heard of. Some were signed by organizations, such as the Sutton State Club of Amarillo.

One telegram, however, was signed by a person Denny knew very well: George Coleman, the chief scout and coach of the redshirts, already in Ohio to watch next week's opponent. Denny blinked at the lines on the yellow sheet of paper: "You've always been a winner in my book, and I know you will be a winner in everyone's book on Saturday."

Denny stacked up the telegrams neatly, folded them, and stuffed them in his jacket pocket. He dropped the envelopes into a large wastebasket in the corner. Then he walked out of the equipment room and headed for the dressing room to change for practice.

In the signal drills, the usual light practice on a

147

Friday before a game, Denny was followed by the whirring television cameras every step of the way.

A van loaded with shouting students appeared on the street next to the practice field. Bumping up over the curb, the van pulled to the sideline, and then went roaring up and down the field, the horn honking and the students shouting. Denny never had seen the van before. He did not know the students. *Denny Fan Club* was painted on one side of the van. *Win with Denny* was painted on the other side.

Ernie Watson, finding himself with new duties every day, was dispatched to chase the van back onto the street and to silence the honking.

After practice, Denny met Paula at the student union for Cokes. They had a standing date for Friday. For the redshirts, Friday was a virtual day off. Even for the varsity, Friday was a day of early quitting time. For Paula, the late afternoon was the last free time before she reported for work at the *Daily Cowboy Times.*

Twice while they sat in the booth people came over asking for autographs.

"Autographs!" Denny blurted in amazement.

Paula grinned at him. "Do you know what you are, Mr. Westbrook?"

"What?"

"You're Mr. Everyman."

"Huh?"

148

"That's right. You are every undersized, untalented fourth-stringer in the world. You are them—the ones who never get to be the star of the game—and they are glorying in every moment of your triumph."

The word *triumph* triggered a thought in Denny's mind. Today's hero had to play a game against Allerton tomorrow. The thought put a frown on his forehead. But he said nothing for a moment. Then he managed a grin. "You editors sure have heavy thoughts, don't you?"

The hour of the pep rally, a Friday night fixture at Sutton State during football season, had arrived.

Standing on the stage of the music shell at the edge of the campus, Denny squinted into the dusk and tried to make out the people in the crowd. He could recognize nobody from this distance in the fading light of the early evening. Then the floodlights came on. He blinked and could see nothing beyond them.

For Denny, this appearance was a first. Never before had the quarterback of the redshirts been invited to join the team onstage for a pep rally. Denny's usual location was out there somewhere on the other side of the footlights, sitting with friends, watching the figures on the stage.

A cheerleader skipped to the center of the stage and shouted into a microphone, "Co-ach Wa-ally Po-olk!"

All around the bandshell, a roaring cheer erupted, rolling like waves over the players standing on the stage.

Wally Polk strode across the stage and took the microphone from the cheerleader. His everyday cowboy outfit had been exchanged for blue slacks and a fancy red shirt with elaborate embroidery and pearl buttons. Polk stood there, motionless, letting the cheers fill the warm autumn evening for a moment. Then he put up a hand, and, as if he had thrown a switch, the cheering ended.

Denny, when he had been sitting in the audience, had often thought Polk's pep-rally talks sounded like an elderly wise man lecturing his beloved children on a point very obvious to him and very important to them.

"We've had a very interesting week," Polk said into the microphone, and he paused.

The laughter rippled around the crowd and then turned into a loud cheer.

"Contrary to what you may have heard, we will be there tomorrow, and we will be there to play our best." Wally Polk never predicted victory, but he always promised "our best." His forecast drew another cheer.

From there, Polk launched into his usual brief technical assessment of the game and then turned to introduce the players. "At the ends . . . Tim Van Buren and Andy Sterling."

150

Tim and Andy stepped forward and waved an acknowledgment of the cheers.

The introductions continued through the tackles, guards, the center, the flanker, the running back, the fullback.

"And our quarterback —"

Polk never got Denny's name out of his mouth. A wild eruption of cheering stopped him in midsentence. For a second, Polk appeared startled. Then he recognized what was happening. He worked his mouth briefly as if determined to pronounce Denny's name anyway. But he gave up. Even the microphone with the amplifier was no match for the thunderous noise rocking the bandshell.

Denny took a step forward. He waved. He smiled. The cheering would not stop. He waved again. Then he thrust his hands in his pockets and stood there, grinning. He felt a little foolish. His heart was pounding rapidly.

At last he stepped back into line, and the cheering began to die out. "For an encore," he told himself, "I am supposed to win tomorrow."

15

The stadium was filling rapidly. All around the giant bowl, home field for the Sutton State Cowboys, the fans streamed up the ramps and climbed the steps to their seats. Most of them wore at least a touch of red —a sweater, a shirt, a jacket, a cap. Many had driven more than 300 miles on unbending interstate highways unbroken by hills to see their Cowboys play. Others had come in by air from points to the east— Houston, Dallas, Fort Worth—jamming the tiny Sutton State airport with row upon row of brightly colored little airplanes. By kickoff, the fans in the stadium would number more than 66,000. Together they formed a giant doughnut of red encircling the playing field. Denny had seen that circle many times, peering up from his spot at the sideline.

The late October sun in the flatlands of West Texas was warm in a cloudless sky that seemed to reach forever. Only the slightest nip in the gentle breeze forecast the autumn weather to come. On the cinder track around the playing field, the television crews—the

152

cameramen mounted on their carts, the sound men with their big dishes for picking up the crowd noise and the sounds of the play on the field—worked themselves into place. In front of the west grandstand, the Sutton State cheerleaders, twenty strong, stepped lightly and clapped their hands in time to the fight song being blared out by the band in the lower seats.

On the field, the Cowboys, in their red jerseys with white numerals, ended their calisthenics and broke out of the lines. They divided into two groups—offense at the west sideline, defense at the east sideline—for their pregame warm-up drills.

The Allerton Lions, wearing white jerseys with green numerals, were at the other end of the field, already running dummy plays.

In front of the Cowboys' bench, now empty, a pair of students in red coveralls lugged a television set into place, a ludicrous sight on a football field for the few who noticed. A gray telephone was riding on top of it. The students put the television set down and looked around, puzzled.

Denny, setting up with the backfield group a few yards away, shouted at the students, "In the center, in the center, behind the bench."

One of the students cupped a hand to his ear, signaling that he could not understand Denny's words above the din of the crowd and the band.

"Just a minute," Denny said to the players around him, and he jogged to the bench.

153

"Right there, behind the bench," he said, pointing to a spot on the grass between the bench and the cinder track.

Denny watched while they located the television set in the proper place and plugged in cables strung across the cinder track—one to the television set, another to the telephone. Then he jogged back to the playing field.

High atop the stadium, on the roof of the press box, Denny saw a television camera being manned by two students in red coveralls. Next to them, two other students, their cameras mounted on tripods, sighted on the field. Other students, probably the runners, were behind them.

Denny glanced at the growing crowd scattered through the stadium. More than half the seats were filled now. Somehow the crowd looked different to Denny on this day. Always before Denny was a part of the crowd. Despite the uniform he wore on the sideline, he was an onlooker, the same as the ticket holders in the grandstand seats. But today he was a participant. Today he was the object of the crowd's attention, not a part of the crowd. The spectators would be watching him. All 66,000 of them would be looking down on him on the playing field. They would see the 12 on his jersey. They would know his name was Denny Westbrook. They would watch him, and they would judge him. Today, for the first time in his

154

life at Sutton State, Denny was separate from the crowd.

Denny turned back to his partners in the backfield. Methodically he moved the offensive unit down the field with a series of dummy plays. Bucky Summers stood at the center of the field, staring impassively at the ritual. Once Wally Polk passed in Denny's line of vision. The coach was striding out to the center of the field to join Summers.

"Hut . . . hut . . . hut . . ." The voice was Denny's now, not a tape recording.

Was the cadence the same? Did he bark the signals today, in the final minutes before the game, the same way he spoke them in the comfort of the studio with Jerry Burton? Or was nervousness making a difference?

As the players turned to reverse their field with the series of dummy plays, Denny stifled a yawn and remembered the dream that had shaken him to wakefulness in the middle of the night.

In the dream, Denny's signal-calling cadence did not matter. His wobbly passes did not matter. His misthrown pitchouts did not matter. Neither did his missteps, his awkward hand-offs, his uncertain running. Nothing mattered because, in the dream, neither Denny nor any other member of the Cowboys' offensive unit ever got into the game. The dream game was a succession of fruitless drives by Allerton, each punc-

155

tuated by a Sutton State touchdown scored by the defense: long punt returns, fumble recoveries in the end zone, long pass interceptions. In the end, Sutton State won the game 66-0, with Denny standing between Earthquake Morrison and Boogie Hadley on the sideline all the way. The offense never got into the game for the first play from scrimmage. Then, at the finish, the players carried Denny off the field on their shoulders.

A whistle sounded and the assistant coaches were waving the players to the dressing room for the final few minutes before the kickoff. Denny turned, jogged to the end of the field, and entered the ramp leading to the dressing room with the crowd of players. They were, as usual, silent as they shuffled through the ramp in the last minutes before the start of the game.

Wally Polk stepped into the center of the dressing-room floor. "I never went into a game I did not think we could win," he said. "And this game is no different."

Around him, the players were seated on benches and training tables, their eyes fixed on the tall figure in cowboy boots, slacks, and an open-neck sport shirt. The thin, gray hair was windblown now, adding somehow to the image of roughhewn sturdiness. His eyes were flashing more than ever. Denny thought, The old man is ready for a fight.

"Louie St. Pierre is not with us today, by his own choice," Polk said. "He decided that breaking the rules last Saturday night was more important to him than playing today with this team."

Hard words, Denny thought. He glanced around the room, but he already knew he would not find Louie St. Pierre in the crowd of players. He wondered idly if Louie were among those in red sitting in the grandstand.

"John Porter and Doug Stephens are out with injuries. That is unfortunate, for them and for the team. Good players are missed."

John, with his crutches, and Doug, his right arm in a sling, stood together at the side of the room.

Denny took his eyes from the coach and stared at the floor. "And so we are left with Westbrook," Denny told himself. He looked back up at the coach.

"Good teams do not quit being good teams because several good players are sidelined," Polk said. "They are weakened, yes, of course, by the loss of good players, but they are still a good team." He glared around the room at the players. He seemed to be daring the players to dispute his statement. He seemed to be demanding understanding and agreement. The glare lasted a full minute. The room was silent.

"I understand the message," Denny told himself. "It's: Let's win this one without Louie St. Pierre. No excuses will be tolerated."

A couple of players nodded unconsciously, as if they had received Wally Polk's message.

"All right, let's go," Polk said.

Earthquake Morrison, near the door, was the first player out. He led the charge of the Cowboys down the ramp and onto the playing field. The Cowboys' fans—all 66,000 of them—leaped to their feet with a roaring cheer, and the band broke into the Cowboys' fight song.

Denny, back in the crowd, moving slowly through the ramp, heard the sudden explosion of noise that greeted the first players racing onto the field.

From behind, he heard, "You okay?"

He turned and saw Boogie Hadley. Denny managed a grin. "Here goes nothing," he said.

On the field, Denny lined up with the starters for the television introductions. He was the last on the list, as the quarterback always is. A camera, riding on the shoulder of a cameraman, was staring at the players past an announcer's shoulder. The announcer was pointing to a spot on the ground where the players were to pause briefly in front of the camera.

Suddenly Denny's mind reeled. This thing was really happening to him. He barely heard the words of the announcer. The roar of the crowd and the noise of the band seemed muted, coming at him from far, far away. His vision blurred briefly. His heart was pounding like a trip-hammer. He had difficulty breathing.

". . . at fullback, Mark Madison."

Denny focused on Mark's back. He saw Mark step into place, pause, and move on. Denny glanced at the

158

announcer. Then he stepped forward. He stopped. He gazed into the camera's eye. He turned and jogged toward the bench, following Mark.

Denny was halfway to the bench before he heard the cheers and the band at full volume again.

Two defensive linemen, designated game captains, marched to the center of the field to meet the Allerton captains for the coin toss. Denny knew their instructions: If we win the toss, we elect to receive the kick-off and let Allerton's Lions pick the goal they want to defend. In good weather, dry and virtually windless, the first possession of the ball was more important than having the choice of goals.

Allerton won the toss and elected to receive.

Denny sighed and stepped back, his helmet in his hand. Fate, in the form of a coin flip, had delayed his debut as a quarterback.

16

Sandy Ruzzo's kick opening the game soared high and straight, backing up the Allerton receiver to the seven-yard line. The kick was perfect. Hanging high, it enabled the Sutton State defenders to charge downfield into position for the tackle before the runner could get under way.

At the sideline, Denny stepped forward. He was holding his helmet in his right hand. He lifted his left hand, shielding the bright sun from his eyes. He watched the ball tumble end over end toward the waiting hands of the Allerton receiver.

The ball fell—and slipped through the receiver's hands.

For a flash of a second, the Allerton player stood unmoving, unable to believe what had happened, unable to react. The Sutton State tacklers were thundering in on him. The ball hit the ground between the receiver's feet and bounded to the right. The receiver came to life suddenly, leaped to his right, grabbed the

160

ball on the bounce, and kept running to his right, moving in a sweeping arc toward the sideline.

Denny, watching, leaned forward. The sudden roar of the crowd at the moment of the fumble settled into a hushed silence. The fans in the grandstand sensed what Denny already knew. The near disaster for Allerton was, in a matter of seconds, being converted into a disaster for Sutton State. The fumble, while frightening and dangerous to Allerton, began working for the Lions the moment the runner scooped up the ball and tucked it away. It was no longer a danger, no longer a disaster; it was an asset. The brief delay in the runner's return was enough to upset the timing of the Cowboy defenders charging downfield. Some tacklers overran him. Others came up short.

At the sideline, the runner picked up a block at the fifteen-yard line. He cut back to the center of the field, running against the grain of the Cowboys' pursuit. He weaved through the tacklers, skillfully taking advantage of what blocking he could find in the open field. He raced to the thirty-five-yard line before a crowd of Cowboys brought him down.

Denny turned away from the field as the teams lined up for the first play from scrimmage. Slowly, almost idly, he walked back to the bench, stepped over it, and approached the television set on its stand. He picked up the telephone on top of it.

Somebody immediately said, "Yeah, what?"

"This thing work?" Denny asked.

"You just wanted our offensive plays, didn't you?"

"Yeah, right."

"We'll have 'em for you."

"Thanks."

Denny hung up the telephone and turned back to the field. The Lions had moved to a first down near the fifty-yard line. Denny saw the officials moving the chains. He stepped over the bench and rejoined the row of players at the sideline.

The Allerton fullback slammed into the line and gained a couple of yards.

Denny remembered his dream: a sixty-minute game with the Sutton State offense never once—not once— taking the field to run a play. A series of fruitless possessions by the Allerton offense eating up the clock, with the defense ending each possession with a touch-down-making turnover: punt returns, pass interceptions, fumble recoveries. Sutton State the 66-0 winner without ever running a play on offense, without Denny Westbrook ever taking the field. And Denny, the victorious quarterback, carried off the field on the shoulders of his teammates.

The Lions, with a short pass over center and an end sweep, got another first down, this time on the Cowboys' thirty-nine-yard line.

"It's my dream come true," Denny mumbled to himself. He could not help smiling at the ridiculous

162

prospect. "Any minute now—interception and touch-down."

"What's that?" John Porter, wearing jeans and a plaid shirt, leaning on his crutches, was standing next to Denny. "What'd you say?"

"Nothing. Just a funny thought."

"I thought you said touchdown."

"We need an interception and a touchdown."

"Oh."

Denny turned his gaze back to the field. But the players were only a blur to him now. Their movements did not register in his mind. His thoughts were on the last words Bucky Summers had spoken to him in the dressing room while he was changing into his uniform.

Usually stone-faced and unemotional, Summers seemed nervous as he ticked off for Denny the points they had discussed over and over during the week. "Call two plays in the huddle right away," he said. "It's bound to surprise 'em. We may get something by starting our play before their defense has time to regroup. And for the rest of the game, their defense will have to wonder—on every play—whether they've got the time to spare to get their defensive signals ready." He smiled slightly, which was when Denny thought the assistant coach seemed nervous. "That was a good idea, Denny, a really good idea."

Then Summers added, "Early on, any passes have

got to be delayed passes—short, delayed passes. Got it?"

Denny nodded. He translated for himself: A shaky quarterback needs a quick measure of success to build confidence—his own confidence in himself and the confidence of his teammates—and a short, delayed pass offered the best chance of success.

"Straight hand-offs. Nothing fancy. No faking. Understand?"

Denny understood. Translation: The Allerton linemen and linebackers will be rushing with reckless abandon in the early minutes against an inexperienced quarterback—to rattle him, nail him, shake his confidence.

In sum, Bucky Summers was saying, "Don't do anything to make yourself look bad in the opening minutes."

For a moment, Denny was sure the assistant coach was actually going to say the words. But he didn't.

"You can do it," Summers said after a moment's silence. The coach's words were not spoken with conviction.

"Yes," Denny said aloud. To himself, he said, "Yes, yes, the vote was six to one."

A sudden roar from the crowd and from the players along the sideline jerked Denny's thoughts back to the game on the field. The ball was in the air, spiraling toward a point on the Cowboys' ten-yard line. An

164

Allerton receiver and a Sutton State defender—it was Lamar Henry—were going up together for the ball.

Denny unconsciously stepped forward with the players around him and peered at the scene developing at the end of the field.

The Lions' receiver and Lamar collided in the air. On the sideline, Denny could hear the pop of the pads as the two players came together at full speed. The Allerton receiver landed on his back. Lamar, clutching the ball in both hands, landed on his feet. For an instant he stumbled. Then he regained his balance. He stood there, holding the ball like a melon in front of him, glancing left and right, sizing up the field. Finally he began running.

Denny turned his gaze to the official, in his black-and-white-striped shirt, poised off to the left of the scene of the collision. The official seemed to reach for the yellow flag in his hip pocket. He was going to pull out the flag and throw it to the ground, signaling a penalty. He was going to call pass interference on Lamar, nullify the interception, and award the Lions the completion on the Cowboys' ten-yard line. The call was a close one, for both players had been going for the ball. Then the official seemed to change his mind. He took his hand away from the pocket—empty—and ran upfield, following Lamar.

A cheer rang out from the sideline.

Denny laughed and shouted, "My dream!" But no

one heard him in the roar of voices around him as Lamar danced his way through the disarray of the Allerton players scattered over the field.

Lamar picked his way carefully through the first of the Lions he encountered. The Lions were off balance and heading the wrong direction. One got a hand on Lamar, then fell away. Lamar seemed to Denny to be moving in slow motion. Somehow he got to the thirty-five-yard line. There he cut to the sideline, zipped to the fifty-yard line right in front of Denny, and seemed to have clear sailing for a touchdown.

Out of the corner of his eye, Denny saw an Allerton player, the last one with a chance of catching Lamar, pumping hard toward Lamar's racing form. He had a good angle for the chase. He was sure to catch him, unless Lamar veered sharply back inside at precisely the right moment. Then the defender's momentum would carry him past Lamar and out of reach. But Lamar had no way of knowing his pursuer's position —or perhaps even his presence—and he did not swerve from his path. The Allerton player caught Lamar and knocked him out-of-bounds at the nine-yard line.

All around Denny the Sutton State players were leaping and shouting and surging toward Lamar, now approaching the bench. Lamar was mobbed. The roaring cheers from the fans in the stadium rolled down onto the field from all sides.

Bucky Summers materialized suddenly next to

Denny. He was not leaping and shouting; he was not even smiling. He was the stone-faced Bucky Summers. "Okay, here we go," he said to Denny with a frown.

Denny nodded. He pulled on his helmet and snapped the chin strap. He jogged onto the field to take up the offense for the Sutton State Cowboys.

"So much for that dream," he said aloud.

17

Denny heard the cheers of the fans and the blaring of the band roaring in his ears as he ran toward the huddle, now setting up around Dutch Hauser near the twenty-yard line. But again the noises were coming to him in a muted way, as if from a long distance away.

Denny leaned into the huddle on one knee. All the faces were turned toward him. This was no practice-field scrimmage. The players were all wearing game jerseys. This time he was not the redshirt quarterback —the walk-on player nobody wanted—calling the plays of next week's opponent to give the defense some practice. He was the Cowboys' quarterback, calling the signals against the Allerton Lions. The crowd was not the smattering of sideline onlookers at the practice field, none of them watching the redshirts anyway. The crowd was 66,000 Sutton State fans. They had come from all over the southwest to see their Cowboys—and to see Denny Westbrook. Denny looked past the huddle at the Allerton defenders in

168

their white jerseys with green numerals. This time they were not his teammates on the field to practice the art of football defense against the redshirts. They were the opponent.

Denny glanced at the faces around him in the huddle: Earthquake Morrison, deadly serious now, with the time for joking behind him. Mike O'Brien, still showing all the signs of anger, frustration, doubt. For Mike, the proof of the mistake was about to become evident. Denny quickly switched his gaze from Mike's face. Dutch Hauser, remembering the fumbled snaps from center. Dutch, like Mike, was sure the time of disaster had arrived. Tim Van Buren, a half smile for Denny, and was that a wink? Boogie Hadley, shifting his weight from one foot to the other as he leaned into the huddle, too excited to stand still.

Probably all of them were expecting Denny to call two plays at once, a quick sequence, so the Cowboys could line up for a quick snap without a huddle, hoping to catch the Allerton defense unready. But Denny realized this place was not the one to spring that particular surprise. On the nine-yard line, the Allerton Lions knew the defense they needed without a lot of consultation. It was goal-line defense. The surprise of moving into a play without a huddle should wait for a midfield situation. There it would pay off. There the defense needed—and expected to get—a few minutes to figure out their strategy. No, the order

169

of the moment was, as Bucky Summers had said, simple, straightforward football, nothing fancy.

Denny called a play that would send Mark Madison plunging from his fullback position between guard and tackle. The play was a basic one. Bucky Summers would approve. He would approve too the choice of the left side of the line. With Dan Graham at guard and Earthquake Morrison at tackle, the left side of the Cowboys' line was awesomely equipped for pushing back defenders.

Nine yards to the goal line. A random thought danced through Denny's mind: How many quarterbacks have put their team into the end zone on the very first play they ever called in a varsity game? The totally irrelevant question brought a half smile to his lips. He was feeling more relaxed than he ever would have imagined. Then he met again the hard stare of Mike O'Brien. His smile faded away.

"Quick-start six," Denny said, dictating a long count for the snap. Perhaps the Lions, overanxious with their backs to the goal, would jump off side. They were sure to be expecting a short count from the new signal caller. A five-yard penalty would be a mighty useful gift at this point. Denny clapped his hands—"Let's go," he said—and the Cowboys broke the huddle.

The team lined up. Denny knelt behind Dutch Hauser. He started to bark the signals. Then he heard the crowd noise. No longer was it muted, no longer

170

did it come from a great distance. The noise was rolling down onto the field from all sides. The sound was deafening.

Denny stepped back and raised his hands. His teammates would not be able to hear the signals in the roaring din.

The referee nodded his acknowledgment of the need for delay to quiet the crowd. If prolonged, the noise could result in a five-yard penalty against the Cowboys for delay of game. Most of the fans surely knew it.

The noise subsided, and Denny stepped back into position. "Hut-hut . . . hut . . . hut . . . hut —"

The referee's whistle interrupted Denny. An Allerton lineman to his right had jumped off side.

Denny straightened up. He turned. He could not help grinning. The long count had worked.

The referee marched off the five-yard penalty and placed the ball down on the Allerton four-yard line. The referee called out, "First down."

In the huddle Earthquake beamed at Denny. "Our quarterback just gained five yards," he announced.

"Same play," Denny said, "on quick-start two. Got that? Quick-start two."

They lined up. Denny called "hut-hut" and took the snap from Dutch. He pivoted on his right foot and extended the ball to his left. Mark Madison charged past at full speed, hands in position. He took in the ball against his stomach. Denny stepped back. Mark slammed into the line between Dan and Earthquake. Dan was muscling an Allerton lineman to the right. Earthquake was shoving one to the left. A hole into the secondary was opening for Mark. The hole was there. Mark ran through. Then Mark stopped. An Allerton linebacker, bent low, his feet spread wide, met Mark with a shoulder in the midsection. Mark spun, legs still churning, trying to roll around and past the linebacker. He needed only an instant of freedom to fall into the end zone. But the linebacker had Mark firmly in his grasp. He held on. The two of them went down together.

A gain of one yard, to the Allerton three-yard line.

Denny took a deep breath. There it was: his first play from scrimmage in a varsity game. He felt a curious mixture of emotions: some disappointment that the play gained only one yard, some disappointment that the play failed to score. Sure, a touchdown on his first play as a varsity quarterback would have been a thrill. Maybe even Mike O'Brien and Dutch Hauser would have softened their glares if he had put the Cowboys in the end zone. And the lead—the lead on the scoreboard—would have been comforting to him in his role of the handicap of his team. But his feeling was also one of relief. There had been no fumble, no misstep, no bad hand-off. The play had been a good one. The Lions had simply stopped it. That was all. Denny sighed as he stepped into the huddle. The sense of relief overcame any disappointment.

On the next play, Denny sent Mark into the other side of the line, over Boogie Hadley at right guard. Boogie moved his man out, and Mark plunged two yards to the Allerton one-yard line before going down in a pile of defenders.

Returning to the huddle, Denny glanced at the sideline. Wally Polk, tall and motionless, stood with his arms folded over his chest, staring at the scene near the goal. Bucky Summers, down the sideline toward the action, was down on one knee, his elbow resting on the other knee, watching impassively. The players were off the bench, standing at the sideline, quietly watching.

Behind the row of players, the slight figure of Sandy Ruzzo was visible. The little kicking specialist was swinging his right foot high in the air. The message was clear: If no touchdown was scored on this next play, Sandy was to come in to try a field goal on fourth down. A three-pointer was not as good as a touchdown, but it was better than nothing.

Bucky Summers was standing now, patting his stomach with his right hand, signaling a plunge into the middle of the line. The play was not what Denny would have called. If left to his own devices, he would have been tempted to try the halfback pass, Mike O'Brien to Tim Van Buren in the end zone. But

Bucky Summers was saying that safety, caution, simplicity remained the catchwords in the early going. Nothing fancy. Not yet.

Denny called the play in the huddle. Down on one knee, he looked up into the faces surrounding him. Each of them registered surprise. Twice the Cowboys had tested the Allerton line. Twice Allerton had stopped the Cowboys short of the goal. Why again? Denny, his mouth a straight line and his forehead creased with a frown, knew the answer: There was no Louie St. Pierre at quarterback to perform a masterful roll-out, or gain a half step for a runner around end with a magical fake into the line, or power himself into the end zone on a quarterback sneak, or fire a rifle shot of a pass into the end zone. There was only Denny Westbrook.

"Let's go," Denny said, clapping his hands.

Mark hit the middle, between Dutch and Dan. He gained nothing.

Denny turned and walked toward the bench. He loosened his chin strap as he went. Already Sandy Ruzzo and Lamar Henry, who held for place-kicks, were coming onto the field.

The walk seemed a long one to Denny. How many steps from failure at the goal line to the bench? He kept his eyes on the ground in front of him. Was he moving at all? He knew the players at the sideline were watching him. He knew the eyes of 66,000 fans were on him. Lamar Henry's spectacular interception,

174

followed by a brilliant run, had presented the Cowboys with a great opportunity. Denny Westbrook's quarterbacking had presented the Cowboys with—nothing. He finally reached the sideline.

His helmet in his hand, Denny stood and watched Sandy kick. The ball sailed end over end through the uprights. On the scoreboard beyond the goalposts the lights blinked: Cowboys 3, Visitors 0. The scoreboard clock showed the game to be five minutes and twenty-one seconds old.

The Lions, far from disheartened at falling behind, came firing back. The telltale sign of high morale and strong determination—good blocking—was evident on the kickoff. The receiver gathered in the ball on the twelve-yard line. This time there was no bobble. He raced straight upfield. An explosion of blocking set him free to the thirty-one-yard line.

Denny could imagine what was in the minds of the Allerton Lions players. Sure, they had given up a field goal and they were trailing on the scoreboard. But they had held the Cowboys at the goal line. They had not yielded a touchdown. And besides, their offense had driven down the field against the Cowboys on their first possession. They could do so again.

Denny turned away from the action on the field. He walked around the end of the row of benches and back up toward the center of the row where the television set stood. He picked up the telephone on top of the television set.

"Westbrook here. Ready?"

From a control room somewhere in the stadium, the voice came back, "Ready. Here she rolls."

Denny turned on the set. The picture flickered to life.

Beside Denny, a figure materialized. It was Bucky Summers. Neither of them spoke. They stared at the television set.

Now looking down on the field from high atop the press box, Denny saw himself jogging onto the field with the other members of the Cowboys' offensive unit. The stunned Lions were trooping to their bench on the other side of the field, meeting their defensive crew coming on. Denny stared at the picture. He had never seen himself on film in a football game before. He found himself in the crowd. The 12 on the back of his jersey was plainly visible. Also, he was the smallest player on the field. He saw himself disappear for a second behind the hulking form of Earthquake Morrison jogging to the huddle.

"Good grief," Denny mumbled. "I *am* small."

Bucky Summers said nothing.

They watched the Allerton lineman jump off side on the first play.

"The long count worked," Summers said. "It may work again, too."

Denny nodded.

On the play sending Mark Madison charging between Dan Graham and Earthquake Morrison

176

through the left side of the line, Denny's eyes widened. On the field, at the moment of the play, he had known only that a linebacker nailed Mark after a one-yard gain. But here on the screen Denny saw that the linebacker had leaped into position at the last second, just before Denny had started his turn with the ball. Blind luck—or maybe instinct—had placed the linebacker in Mark's path. If the linebacker had held his position or had jumped the other way, Mark would have scored.

"Look at that," Denny said.

"Uh-huh."

"If he had jumped the other way. . . ."

"He will, before the game is over," Summers said.

Denny glanced at the coach. He understood now the reason for the signal to send Mark into the middle on third down. The reason was not the absence of Louie St. Pierre. It was the very good chance that the play would work.

They watched Mark plunge through the hole opened by Boogie Hadley on the second play. A blocked-out lineman spun away and got himself back into the play, catching Mark after two yards. There was no stopping that kind of second effort. The Allerton lineman had made a brilliant play. He deserved the tackle.

A student in red coveralls, a sideline pass dangling on a chain around his neck, rushed up to Denny and handed him a sheaf of Polariod photographs.

177

"Thanks," Denny said, keeping his eye on the television screen.

He was pivoting now, handing off to Mark for the third-down plunge into the center of the line from the one-yard line. Mark hit a wall of people and stopped. The entire Allerton defense seemed to be waiting for him.

But no, not the entire Allerton defense. Denny spotted the defensive halfbacks in the end zone, lying back, then dashing up to meet Mike O'Brien and Tim Van Buren as they circled into the end zone as decoys. A pass would have had tough going and little chance of success.

A bit sheepishly Denny said, "I wanted to try Mike's halfback pass on that play."

Summers gave Denny a tight little smile. "Plenty of time for that," he said.

18

On the field, the Lions were moving the ball against the Cowboys.

Denny, standing at the television set thumbing through the collection of Polaroid pictures, heard the roar of a home crowd alarmed. He looked around in time to see an Allerton back gallop around end, deftly cut back inside, and romp over the fifty-yard line into Sutton State territory.

He laid the pictures in a neat stack on top of the television set and weighted them down with the telephone. The pictures had shown him little. The Lions' goal-line defense was predictable. Later, Denny knew, when the pictures revealed the spread of the defense at midfield, he would find chinks in the armor by looking at them. They would show the route for him to take to gain a yard, or a first down—or a touchdown.

Denny walked from the television set around the row of benches and took up a position in the line of players standing at the sideline. To his left, Wally Polk, holding a legal-size writing pad in his hand, was barking something above the crowd noise into the ear of a substitute ready to take the field. The instructions obviously involved a defensive adjustment aimed at halting the march of the Lions.

"What's happening?"

Tim Van Buren looked irritated. "What? Where have you been?"

Denny grinned at the lanky receiver, shrugged, and said, "I've been over there watching television."

"Oh."

"They're really moving the ball," Denny said.

"They sure are. Three straight first downs."

A quick sideline pass carried the Lions to their fourth straight first down, moving them to the Cowboys' thirty-yard line.

The quiet of the crowd in the stadium told Denny as surely as the position of the ball on the field that the Cowboys were in trouble. Gone were the shouts of alarm at a big play. The Lions were pressing close to the Cowboys' goal, and the crowd settled into a hushed silence.

Denny had sensed problems to come when he watched the slashing blocks that sprang the runner loose on the kickoff return. Now the Lions were dominating the game. They were in the midst of the most fearsome of all sights in a football game—a sustained drive. They were eating up yards, moving toward the goal. And, almost equally bad, they were running off the clock with their second long possession of the ball.

The more time the Lions held the ball, the less time the Cowboys had it for their own plays. And the Cowboys, crippled at quarterback, needed all the chances they could get. Nobody on the Cowboys' side of the field was smiling.

On the field, Lamar Henry was waving a partner at defensive halfback over to the side.

The Lions' quarterback took the snap from center. He stepped back. He pivoted easily. He faked to a back plunging into the line. The move, as designed, froze the Sutton State linebackers in their tracks. The quarterback straightened suddenly and rifled a pass to a flanker coming out of the backfield. The flanker was on the sideline, eight yards down the field. The bullet pass hit its target. The Cowboys' defensive halfback, unable to reach the ball for deflection, slammed himself into the receiver, knocking him out-of-bounds.

The gain carried the Lions to the Cowboys' twenty-two-yard line. It was second down and two to go for another first down.

Denny could not help admiring the Allerton quarterback. He was no match for the talents of Louie St. Pierre. But he was an able ball handler and a superb passer. He was engineering the Lions' drive down the field—a plunge, a pass, an end run, another pass—with a deadly effectiveness.

On the next play, the quarterback zipped a low sidearm pass over center into the end zone for a touchdown.

Moments later the scoreboard showed: Cowboys 3, Visitors 7.

While the teams lined up for the kickoff, Denny walked down the line and stood next to Bucky Summers.

"If Richie gets the kickoff back past the thirty-yard line, try the halfback pass," Summers said. "On first down, it may catch them off balance. Either way it will help Mike on end runs. After they've seen the halfback pass, they won't be able to assume that he's running every time he takes off around end."

Denny nodded.

"And this may be the time to go without a huddle. But —"

"I know," Denny said. "Not after a long gainer."

"Yeah, okay."

Denny himself had pointed out, when he first suggested calling two plays in the huddle, that the strategy would not pay off after a long gain on the first play. A long gain left players strung out over the field, unable to take up their positions on the line of scrimmage quickly. To be effective, running a play without a huddle needed a quick snap when all players were on their proper side of the line and the defense was expecting an offensive huddle and a few seconds to regroup.

The Allerton kickoff was low but long, backing Richie to the eight-yard line. Richie took in the ball

182

and looked upfield. He had time to maneuver. The low line drive of the kick lacked the hang time the defenders needed to run downfield for the tackle. In front of Richie, the Cowboys' blocking formed. Richie charged straight ahead, up the center of the field, into the crowd of blockers gathering for him. For a moment, he disappeared in the churning mass of play-ers—the red jerseys of Sutton State, the white jerseys of Allerton. Then he burst out the other side, on his feet, stumbling, and fell in the arms of a tackler on the thirty-two-yard line.

Denny jogged onto the field, snapping the chin strap of his helmet.

Down on one knee, leaning into the huddle, he looked straight into Mike O'Brien's eyes. "Let's do the halfback pass," he said. Mike nodded. Denny turned to Tim. "Get yourself open. Here it comes." Tim nodded solemnly.

"Quick-two for the snap," Denny said, figuring Allerton's line would be braced for another long count, having been caught once for an off-side pen-alty.

The teams lined up. Denny knelt behind Dutch. He looked over the line into the eyes of the Allerton line-backer. The linebacker, four yards away, was rocking on the balls of his feet, arms hanging loose, staring into Denny's eyes. Denny knew the strategy: intimida-tion. The linebacker figured that it could work on a new quarterback, who was a fourth-stringer, of all things. What frightened Denny more than the threat of the linebacker was the fact that the tactic had almost succeeded. Denny caught himself thinking about the linebacker instead of concentrating on the play at hand. He came close to unconsciously adjusting his stance behind Dutch Hauser. The movement of one foot would be illegal motion—a five-yard penalty against the Cowboys. Denny looked past the linebacker, staring blankly into space, and kept his feet planted on the ground.

"Hut-hut."

He took the snap from Dutch. He swung his left foot back, pivoting on his right, and slipped the ball forward into Mark Madison's stomach. Then he withdrew the ball. Mark, bending low and clutching his stomach, charged into the line, faking a plunge. Denny took another step back. He was holding the ball on his thigh. He turned and sent an underhanded pass to Mike, racing out to the left.

Denny was watching Mike as he shoveled the ball away. Mike was running hard, looking back for the ball. Denny could see Mike's eyes flashing and his jaw clenched tightly. His hands were extended, the fingers splayed.

Denny felt a strange sensation the moment the ball left his hand. His part of the play was completed. He had taken the snap from center—no fumble. He had executed the fake to Mark—no fumble. He had turned with the ball on his thigh—no fumble. And now he had pitched out to Mike. The sensation was thrilling; the play was working.

But the pitchout was far from perfect. With a sinking feeling, Denny saw he had failed to lead Mike sufficiently. The ball was coming in behind Mike—only slightly, but enough to give trouble.

Denny danced wildly from one foot to another. He tried, through body English, to change the course of the pitchout, to send the ball farther out in front of Mike. It didn't work.

Mike slowed, reached back, and caught the ball. He tucked it away for the run.

Denny blew out a large breath of air. "Whew!"

The Allerton defenders were sweeping to Denny's left in pursuit of Mike heading around end. Suddenly Mike screeched to a halt. He looked straight ahead. He brought up the ball. Then he looked to his right, across the field, seeking Tim. He cocked his arm. He fired.

Tim, alone at the far sideline, took the pass flat-footedly. He was at the forty-three-yard line. He sidestepped an Allerton defender plunging toward him. The Allerton player crashed to the ground, out-of-bounds. Tim took off.

All over the field the Allerton players were slamming on the brakes. They were turning to follow the course of the ball. They were taking off toward the slender figure with the ball, now crossing the fifty-yard line. Gradually they closed in on Tim.

Spinning, wriggling, driving forward, Tim fought his way to the Allerton thirty-seven-yard line before going down beneath a couple of Allerton tacklers.

Denny, jogging to the huddle, heard the roar of the crowd and the beat of the Sutton State band blaring from the stands. Louder still, he heard the beating of his own heart. He recalled the predawn scribbling at the study table in the dormitory where the play had been born. "It worked. It worked," he told himself. Downfield, the Cowboys were slapping Tim and Mike on the back as they moved toward the huddle.

Denny glanced at the sideline markers. The thirty-seven-yard line. A bit too much of a kick for Sandy. The little kicking specialist was deadly accurate within his range. But he was no powerhouse. He needed to be closer. So even to hope for a field goal, if not a touchdown, Denny had to propel the Cowboys at least another fifteen yards downfield.

At the huddle, Denny remembered Bucky Summers' statement that the halfback pass would make Mike's end runs all the more dangerous. The Allerton defenders could not charge forward recklessly when Mike started around end. After all, he might be passing again. They would have to play him cautiously. And Mike was capable of running circles around their caution. So why not?

186

Denny called the play—same play, only this time Mike was to keep going, racing around end, while the Allerton defenders wondered if he was passing again.

Breaking the huddle, Mike said to Denny, "Lead me this time, will you?"

Denny nodded and stepped up behind Dutch for the snap.

The play was the same: the snap, the fake to Mark into the middle of the line, the turning with the ball on his hip, the underhanded shovel pass to Mike. But the pass was better this time.

Mike took in the pitchout at full speed. He tucked the ball away. He raced out wide. The Allerton defenders, seeing the exact same play coming at them again, hesitated. It was not possible. No team would try the same halfback pass play twice in a row. But it was happening. Or was he running with the ball this time?

By the time the Allerton defenders recovered and brought themselves to the correct conclusion, Mike was dancing down the sideline, utilizing the speed that made him one of the most dangerous runners in collegiate football. At the sixteen-yard line, Mike was shoved out-of-bounds.

"Two plays," Denny said in the huddle. He called for Richie Carson to race wide around the right end, and then for Mark Madison to plunge between Dan and Earthquake in the left side of the line. A plunge, developing quickly, seemed to Denny to offer the greatest chance of a big gain against an unready defense. "Remember: Line up quick. Get into your stance quick."

Kneeling behind Dutch, Denny gazed into the end zone. It was only sixteen yards away. It looked empty, so very attainable.

"Hut-hut . . . hut-hut."

Denny took the snap, turned, made a short pitch to Richie. The pitch seemed good. But Richie juggled the ball momentarily. He slowed himself to gain control of the ball. A linebacker shot through and slammed Richie to the ground four yards behind the line of scrimmage.

A low moan rolled down onto the field from the grandstands.

But to Denny, the loss was not entirely bad news. It meant the referee would be placing the ball at a spot that left virtually all the Allerton defenders already on their own side of the line of scrimmage. There would be no waiting for players to cross the line to their proper positions.

The Cowboys moved into position. The last of the Allerton players—the one who had tackled Richie—was now on his side of the line. Denny knelt behind Dutch.

Somebody on the Allerton side shouted the alarm. "Hey!"

Dutch snapped the ball. Denny turned and handed the ball to Mark. Mark hit the gap between Dan and

188

Earthquake. He slashed forward for seven yards, no more.

Denny slammed his right fist into the palm of his left hand. Third down and seven to go for a first down.

Mike got five yards knifing off tackle, and Sandy Ruzzo trotted onto the field with Lamar Henry. Denny walked to the sideline.

Sandy's kick was good: Cowboys 6, Visitors 7.

19

The waning minutes of the first quarter ticked away. Then the second quarter settled into a series of fruitless tests—all between the thirty-yard lines—for both teams.

The Cowboys' defense, so porous during the first two Allerton drives, stiffened and plugged the gaps. Wally Polk's defensive adjustments were working. The players were pushing hard for the one added step, the extra bit of effort. The combination spelled success. The Allerton runners were stopped. The Allerton passes were knocked down. Twice the Allerton quarterback was caught for big losses trying to pass. The Allerton attack, after appearing unstoppable in the first two drives, was reduced to a sputtering machine in the face of the Cowboys' revived and revised defense.

But the Cowboys' offense wasn't going anywhere either. Mark Madison's plunges were gaining one, three, or five yards. The end runs by Mike and Richie were picking up half a dozen yards at the best, but not

190

often enough. Sometimes they were stopped cold, and twice they were thrown for losses. Calling two plays in the huddle was a big help. The Allerton defense never was quite ready. Denny's varying his cadence—"hut-hut . . . hut"—was a help too. Twice more the Cowboys gained five yards on off-side penalties. The halfback pass had more than earned its way. Not only had the pass been a big gainer, it forced the Allerton defenders to view Mike as a double threat, which was a big help. But still, the Cowboys were unable to mount a sustained drive. They could not put together the good moves, the good gains, the good breaks in the necessary sequence for a score. The attack lacked consistency.

Denny knew what was needed: a passing quarterback. Only a few passes—dangerous and effective—were needed to loosen the Allerton defense, opening the way for the runners. As it was, the Allerton defenders keyed on the runners, Mark, Mike, and Richie. Once Denny threw a pass—wobbly, floating, off-target, almost intercepted. He returned to the straight hand-offs and the standard pitchouts.

All around the stadium the Sutton State fans were quiet. Their Cowboys, a national power, were trailing on the scoreboard. Worse yet, they were settling into a drab, punchless, lackluster attack. The one spark of the attack—the halfback pass—had led to a field goal, nothing more. And there had been no more sparks.

The ghost of Louie St. Pierre seemed everywhere. More than Louie's skill was missing. True, the Cowboys were a weaker team without Louie's pinpoint passing. And they were weaker without his scrambling runs. But in addition, the Cowboys were missing the simple threat of Louie's presence on the field. Mark Madison's function as a thundering fullback was less productive because the Allerton defense, unworried about the quarterback, concentrated on nailing Mark at the line of scrimmage. Mike O'Brien and Richie Carson were less dangerous, skittering around the ends, because the Allerton defense, unworried about the quarterback, was going after them without a second thought.

Time and again in the huddle, Denny saw reactions to his shortcomings stamped on the expressions of his teammates. Mark, overworked and breathing heavily, shrugged when his number was called yet another time. Mike's face clearly said, "I told you so." Dutch Hauser grunted and nodded and kept his eyes on the ground. He was fighting a tough battle blocking in the center of the line. But for what? Even Earthquake Morrison and Tim Van Buren, who were Denny's friends and supporters, were wearing worried looks. The frowns were deepening all around the huddle as the frustration dragged on through the second quarter.

Still, Denny remained optimistic. Alone among them all, Denny was sure the game plan was right on

192

track, moving along as scheduled. Sure, it would be better if the Cowboys had been able to convert their two scoring opportunities into touchdowns instead of field goals. It would be better to be leading 14-7 instead of trailing 7-6. The scowls in the huddle would not be there if the Cowboys were riding a one-touchdown lead. Denny blamed himself. The fact was inescapable: The Cowboys' quarterback had been unable to get them into the end zone when it counted. But Denny knew, as the rest of them should remember, that there were some tricks still in the bag, as yet unrevealed. And Denny knew, as none of the rest of them could possibly know, that the frustrations of the second quarter might pay big dividends in the third and fourth quarters. He knew what he had seen on the television screen and in the Polaroid pictures.

In between the ineffectual efforts on the field, Denny stood behind the row of benches staring at the flickering figures on the television screen and studying the photographs. Most of the time Bucky Summers stood with him, pointing out the tendencies of the Allerton defense, the flaws at a given position, the possibilities that were opening up for the Cowboys.

From time to time, other players—usually Tim, occasionally Richie, once even Mike—gathered around and looked at the videotape replays of themselves in action. Denny was watching neither himself nor his teammates. He was watching the Allerton defenders.

193

The dreadful three-plays-and-punt strategy of the Cowboys yielded an obvious point of interest for Denny. "They're charging on the punts like there was no tomorrow," Denny said.

"They sure are," Bucky Summers agreed.

Denny grinned. "They'll charge once too often," he said, "and tomorrow will be ours." He could see in his mind a couple of well-placed blocks springing Mike or Mark loose for a long gain—perhaps a touchdown —on a fake punt.

Increasingly, the Lions were bunching themselves up tight to the line of scrimmage and zeroing in on the runners, especially on third down. With each play, their confidence in the tactic was growing. And why not? The tactic was working. They were certain nothing fancy—not even a pass from the quarterback —was coming. There was going to be a run for sure: Mark into the line, or Mike or Richie around the ends.

"There, right there," Denny said suddenly. "Look at them! Nobody's back. They're all pressed up front, ready to rush. A quick kick would bounce forever."

Summers nodded. "Yeah," he said, "and any kind of pass over center would work—any kind."

Denny glanced at the coach. "Any kind?" he asked with a devilish grin. "You mean, even my kind of pass?"

Summers grunted in reply and wandered away.

Even more than the videotape replays, the sequence

194

of Polariod pictures, stacked neatly in the order of arrival, showed a growing weakness on the part of the Allerton defense. In many ways, a still picture was more revealing than the fleeting glimpse of leaping figures in motion pictures. Denny, studying the pictures, laughed when he saw the first picture of himself being completely ignored by the onrushing Allerton defenders.

"Look at that," he said to Tim. "Not a one of them is even looking at me. Now that's what I call something to damage your ego."

Tim leaned over and looked at the picture. He shrugged. "You've already given the ball away. You're out of the play. Nobody cares about the quarterback after he's handed off."

But then, time and again, as Denny scanned the pictures, he found himself to be the object of no attention at all whether he had the ball or not. The Allerton defenders were concentrating entirely on the player with the ball or the player they thought was going to receive the ball. Denny wasn't passing. Denny wasn't running. Why bother?

"That's interesting," Denny mumbled to himself.

The dressing room at half time was, as always, busy but subdued. It was like a beehive, with the volume of the buzzing turned down, reduced to slow-motion activity. There was work to be done and limited time. Nobody wasted a move or a word. Trainers moved

195

among the players, inspecting bruises, checking the strips of tape, testing knees and ankles. Nobody seemed to be speaking, but the low hum of voices could be heard. At one side of the room, in front of a blackboard, an assistant coach drew x's and o's and squiggly lines to show the defensive players how they must react in the second half.

At the front of the room, Wally Polk and Bucky Summers were talking. Polk waved Denny over. Mike, Tim, and Mark trailed behind Denny.

"Now's the time to open it up," Polk said.

"Open it up!" Mike blurted. He blushed when Polk glared at him.

Denny stared at the floor, embarrassed for Mike. He knew what Mike thought of him as a football player. He knew what Mike thought of Wally Polk's decision to play Denny. But he knew too that Wally Polk would brook no objections from his players—not last week, not today, not ever.

The other players shuffled their feet.

Polk continued as if nothing had been said. "Over there in the Allerton dressing room, they're talking about what they saw in the first half—the surprises: the staggered count, the halfback pass, the quick snap without a huddle. If it had not been for those things, we would be trailing 7-0 instead of 7-6. And we've not used everything we've got." He paused and glanced at Mike.

"We've got the quick kick. Let's use it. We've got

196

the fake punt. Let's use it. We've got the halfback pass, and it'll work again before this game is over. Bet on it. And Denny"—Polk turned to face Denny—"they're leaving themselves wide open for a short pass over center. You know the play—Tim or Andy, five yards over the line. Use it. Just throw it up there."

Denny nodded. His mind went back to his one aerial effort of the first half–a wobbly floater that an Allerton player almost grabbed off for an interception.

"In the Allerton dressing room, a coach is telling the defense right now to watch out for that kind of pass," Polk said. "Their coaches can see the opening as well as we can. But the Allerton players won't believe him. The opening still will be there. Just throw it up there."

Denny nodded.

Then Polk almost grinned and added, "It doesn't matter if it wobbles."

Denny shrugged. "That's good," he said.

Denny and the others retreated to benches and sat down, taking a moment to relax. Denny wished the half-time intermission would end. He wanted to get the second half under way. He felt, more than anyone around him could imagine, that he had the tools to win the game. The talent was there—Mike, Earthquake, Tim, all of them. The surprises in his bag of tricks were enough, he was sure, to make up for the weak link at quarterback. Enough, that is, if used at

197

precisely the right moment, in exactly the right situation. He was anxious to get at the task.

Finally Ernie Watson, in his big moment at the end of half time, came walking through the dressing room announcing in his brisk tones, "Time. Time to go. Time."

20

Denny dropped to one knee and leaned into the huddle.

The third quarter was half gone. Once again the Cowboys' strong defense had stopped the Lions and forced them to punt. The ball was on the Cowboys' forty-five-yard line. It was first down.

Denny looked at the faces in the huddle around him and called the play: a short pass over center. Expressions of surprise and doubt were all around Denny. His one wobbly pass of the game had nearly been a disaster. A wobbly floater here, giving the Lions an interception, could well seal the Cowboys' fate. But on the television screen and in the Polaroid pictures, Denny had seen the Allerton defenders ignoring him. They just knew that the little quarterback with the number 12 on his back was going to hand off or pitch out the ball. They just knew that he was not going to run or try a pass. Wally Polk had said, "Just throw it up there." So he was going to do so. "Let's surprise 'em," Denny said, clapping his hands and breaking the huddle. And, walking into position at the line of scrimmage, he said to himself, "And surprise me, too, if it works."

Denny paused for a moment behind Dutch before signaling for the snap. He looked at the Allerton linebacker in front of him. The linebacker, having seen only the one shaky pass from Denny through the entire game, was getting careless. He was poised to chase a runner. Now was the time for the linebacker to pay the penalty for his carelessness. Denny glanced to his right. Tim was settling into his split-end position, ready to race over the center, five yards beyond the line of scrimmage. Fearful that his glance at Tim might have tipped the play, Denny deliberately turned and looked at Mike O'Brien, in position at the flanker spot to his left.

"Hut . . . hut . . . hut."

Denny took the snap. He stepped back. He straightened. Tim was a red blur moving from right to left in front of him. He cocked his arm and he threw. Somebody smacked into him and knocked him down. On the ground he heard the roar of the crowd. By the time he rolled over and leaped to his feet, he was alone. The action was downfield.

Denny located Tim, just going down under a tackler near the sideline, almost to the Lions' forty-yard line.

Denny shot a fist into the air and ran to the huddle taking shape just over the fifty-yard line.

Tim was grinning.

"Right on the button, huh?" Denny asked with a laugh. "It's the aerial circus of slingin' Denny Westbrook, huh?"

Tim rolled his eyes. "Don't ask," he said.

Denny called two plays—Mark through the middle and then the halfback pass. Mark got four yards, leaving the Cowboys with second down and six to go.

Despite the quick lineup without a huddle, the Lions were ready. They seemed to sense what was coming. When Denny took the snap, the defenders swarmed around Tim coming off the line of scrimmage. Ducking and weaving, Tim tried to free himself. He couldn't. Mike, with the pitchout, had completed his fake run. He was trying to pass to Tim. He waited as long as he dared. Then he tucked the ball away to make a run for it. But he had waited too long. Three Lions were thundering in on him. Mike gave a quick fake to his left. The tacklers swerved momentarily. The move gave Mike a half-step advantage. He whirled to his right, reversing his field, and took off in a sweeping arc trying to run against the grain of the defense. Denny threw himself in front of one of the tacklers, leveling him. Mike, yielding yardage in his race for the sideline, picked up a couple of other blockers. He suddenly made the cut upfield. Then out of nowhere a tackler knifed through and drove Mike to the ground.

The play was an eight-yard loss. Now the Cowboys

faced third down and fourteen yards to go for a first down. They were on the Lions' forty-four-yard line.

Denny moved to the huddle slowly. He knew that a pass was needed on third down with fourteen yards to go. But a team had to have a passer to function properly on a passing down. The halfback pass, despite Wally Polk's confidence, was not working at this point. Denny toyed with the idea of another short pass over center to Tim. No, the Lions would be watching for it this time. Denny considered a straight pass play. Just send out Mike and Tim in their normal patterns and throw the ball to one of them. Pretty simple. But the memory of Denny's earlier attempt sent a shudder through him. So much for the aerial circus of slingin' Denny Westbrook.

At the sideline, Bucky Summers stood motionless, his hand resting on his stomach.

Denny got the signal: Mark Madison into the middle of the line. Denny could not argue. He had no better ideas.

Mark, fighting hard, got four yards against a defense that was waiting for him.

Denny turned and saw, for what seemed the hundredth time, the slender figure of the punter, Ralph Lawrence, jogging onto the field. Tim went to the bench to make room in the lineup for the punter.

Denny gave Ralph a questioning glance as he approached.

"Fake punt," Ralph said softly.

"Yeah."

In the huddle, Denny called the play. He looked at Mark. "You okay?" The fullback had taken a battering all afternoon. He was breathing heavily from the last charge into the middle of the line.

"Okay," Mark panted.

The teams lined up. On signal, the Cowboys shifted into punt formation. Ralph dropped back to take the snap. Denny stepped back and to the right, taking up a blocking position. Mark stationed himself in front of Ralph and to the left, poised to block.

Dutch's snap of the ball—to Mark, not Ralph—was perfect. It was a low spiral, slightly to the left of Mark, leading him in the direction he was to run. Mark took in the ball smoothly and shifted into high gear, heading for the sideline. Behind him, Ralph went through the motions of punting.

The play caught the Lions flat-footed. Completely taken in, the Lions were charging in an attempt to block the punt. They had nine players in the rush.

Mark, in his first half-dozen strides, left most of the Allerton defense behind him. The Allerton punt returner, recovering from his surprise, rushed up to meet Mark. A defensive halfback was racing across the field to try to intercept him. In the line, the Lions thrashed around in confusion. Then they discovered the trick. One by one they looked around, saw what was happening, and tried to untangle themselves to join the pursuit.

Mark was crossing the thirty-yard line. He had the first down. He was still going. He veered back toward the center of the field and escaped the punt returner moving up for the tackle. He was past the twenty-five-yard line. From the side, the defensive halfback caught up with Mark. He slammed him to the ground at the twenty-one-yard line.

Denny, running downfield, shot his fists into the air.

From the twenty-one-yard line, Denny sent Mike out wide for a four-yard gain, pitched out to Richie Carson to the right for no gain, and sent Mike off tackle for two yards.

With fourth down and four yards to go for a first down, on the Lions' fifteen-yard line, Sandy Ruzzo and Lamar Henry jogged onto the field and Denny turned and walked off.

Denny walked straight to the television set. He lifted the phone and was telling the control room to roll the picture when the roar from the crowd told him that Sandy's kick was good. Denny turned and watched the scoreboard change: Cowboys 9, Visitors 7.

"We're out front," an elated voice came singing through the telephone.

"It's not over yet," Denny said. "Let me have the picture."

Denny watched the screen, stopping the projection only once for a replay. He wanted a second look at his short pass over center to Tim. He frowned as he stared at the scene. He had thrown off balance, his weight on the wrong foot. The pass was more of a shove than a throw. He failed to lead Tim sufficiently. Tim had to slow himself and reach back to grab the ball. The catch was miraculous.

"Not exactly your picture-book passer," Denny mumbled.

But Denny found in the scene the encouraging sign he was seeking. The play confirmed again that the Allerton defenders were paying hardly any attention to Denny. Even the player who smacked Denny to the ground seemed unaware—or uncaring—that Denny was trying to pass. The collision seemed more an accident, an inadvertent bump delivered en route to another assignment.

Even after the pass, when Mark plunged into the line and then when Mike tried the halfback pass, the Allerton players ignored Denny in their pursuit of the ball. They seemed to consider Denny's pass an aberration, a quirk, a onetime thing, unlikely to recur.

The fake punt was a thing of beauty. Every last one of the Allerton defenders had been fooled. Even the punt receiver, standing back and watching the play unfold in front of him, had been slow to react. Denny made a mental note that the fake punt might work again.

A runner in red coveralls appeared at Denny's side and handed him a stack of Polaroid pictures. Denny accepted them without taking his eyes off the screen.

The videotape was approaching the point he really wanted to see. Less exciting than his pass over center, less spectacular than the fake punt, the last three probes at the Allerton defense were going to answer a big question for Denny.

Denny nodded absently as he watched the screen: Mike circling left end for four yards, Richie going down for no gain on the right side, Mike plunging off tackle for two yards. The Allerton defenders were, indeed, ignoring Denny completely.

Denny knelt on the grass and spread out the Polaroid pictures on the ground.

Suddenly a roar from the crowd brought Denny to his feet. He could not see the field past the row of players standing at the sideline. He stepped up on the bench and stared out over the field.

Just as Denny located the action, the ball—a long pass—was dropping into the hands of an Allerton receiver at the fifteen-yard line. The Allerton receiver had a one-step advantage over Lamar Henry. The pass was right on target. The receiver took in the ball without breaking stride. Lamar lunged toward him. The receiver cut sharply to his right. Lamar crashed to the ground, empty-handed. The receiver raced into the end zone.

21

The scoreboard showed the bad news: Cowboys 9, Visitors 14. The fourth quarter was one minute old.

Denny knelt at the sideline, his helmet in his hand, and watched as the teams lined up on the field for Allerton to kick off to the Cowboys.

The bits and pieces of information Denny had absorbed in the last hour and a half paraded through his mind. The little things—but now important—ticked by. There was the Allerton linebacker, given to leaping to one side or the other at the last moment, trying to anticipate the hole the Cowboys were sending the ball through. If correct, he made a great defensive play. If mistaken, he left a channel open through which the Cowboys could gallop to big yardage. He was right more often than wrong. But Denny reminded himself that the linebacker was not right every time. There was the lineman opposite Earthquake, not only beaten but intimidated at this stage of the game. Earthquake had made his opponent a weak link in the chain of the Allerton defense. Denny made

207

a mental note that Mark's plunges should go into the left side of the line. There was the Allerton secondary, covering Tim like a blanket every time he looped out toward the sideline. Wally Polk had predicted that the halfback pass would work again. But it wouldn't, and Denny knew it. There was the entire Allerton defense, ignoring Denny, certain he would not pass, certain he would not run. Denny had seen these things on the field. He had seen them on the television screen. He had seen them in the Polaroid pictures. Now, out of the conglomeration of facts must come the recipe for a touchdown.

The time had passed for field goals. To put the Cowboys above the Lions on the scoreboard would take two of Sandy Ruzzo's perfect kicks. There was only the slimmest of chances the Cowboys could put the ball in position twice, not once, for field goals in the fourth quarter. Also, even if they did, there always was the chance of Sandy missing. No, the Cowboys had to have a touchdown. Denny had to think touchdown.

Richie took in the kickoff on the ten-yard line. Racing straight up the middle, twisting and turning, he scampered to the thirty-two-yard line.

Denny put on his helmet, snapped the chin strap in place, and jogged onto the field. On the first play, he handed off to Mark into the left side of the line. Earthquake shoved his opponent to the left, and Mark shot through the hole. The linebacker jumped the wrong way. A half step out of position, he tried to move in front of Earthquake to get a hand on Mark. Earthquake flattened him just as Mark veered to the right and angled out through the secondary.

The Allerton defenders finally dragged Mark to the ground on the forty-four-yard line—a twelve-yard gain and a first down. Denny clapped his hands as he raced toward the huddle.

A run around right end by Mike got four yards, a run to the left by Mike got two, a plunge by Mark got one, and Denny looked up, again facing fourth down. They were three yards short of the first down, with the ball resting on the Allerton forty-nine-yard line. The Cowboys had crossed the fifty-yard line. But there were no points awarded for crossing the fifty.

For a brief moment, Denny wanted to go for it. Mark, charging behind the broad back of Earthquake, might make the needed three yards. The drive would stay alive. With time running out, a gamble was needed—a winning gamble.

But then he saw Ralph Lawrence trotting onto the field to punt. For Wally Polk, it was not late enough to resort to desperate gambles.

At the sideline, for the first time in the game, Denny stood and watched the play on the field. The time for studying the television screen was past. The time for scrutinizing Polaroid pictures was past. The lessons to be learned had been learned by now. All that remained was the fact that the Cowboys had a little

209

more than ten minutes to score a touchdown. Denny took off his helmet and stood in the row of silent players at the sideline.

For five minutes the Allerton Lions churned slowly down the field—three yards on a plunge, two yards on an end run—marking up one, two, three first downs, letting the clock run. Finally, on third down and three at the Allerton forty-eight-yard line, the Cowboys stopped them cold, and the Allerton punter entered the game.

Denny glanced at the yardage situation: midfield. And he glanced at the clock: a little over five minutes of playing time remaining. His heart sank. Even a short punt would leave the Cowboys facing an enormous expanse of the playing field to cover and precious little time to do so.

The punt was in the air when Denny stepped out of the line of players at the sideline and started looking for the tall figure of Wally Polk. When Denny spotted the coach, Polk was not watching the play on the field. He was looking at Denny. He waved the legal-size pad he carried in his hand. Denny raced down the sideline toward him.

Together they said the same words, "The quick kick."

A quick kick was the only play to back the Lions up against their goal. With luck, the Cowboys racing downfield to cover the kick might force a fumble. But in any case, the Lions would be deep in their own territory, and the Cowboys would have five minutes to wrest the ball away and score.

Richie took in the punt on the Cowboys' eighteen-yard line. He swept to the right side, picked up a couple of blockers, and battled his way to the thirty-two-yard line.

Denny and the other members of the offensive unit raced onto the field. Mike hit right tackle for two yards. Then Denny called two plays in the huddle—Mark over left tackle, behind Earthquake, and then, if Mark fell short of a first down, a quick lineup and a quick kick.

Mark struggled four yards to the thirty-eight-yard line.

The Allerton players lumbered back toward their positions to take up the defense for the next play. They were in no hurry. They wanted the clock to run as much as possible between plays.

"Hut . . . hut."

Dutch sent the ball spiraling through Denny's legs. Denny shoved hard on Dutch, joining in the effort to block. From behind, he heard the sound—*thuh-umph!*—of Mark putting his foot to the ball.

Somebody on the Allerton side of the line shouted, "Quick kick."

Denny looked up. The ball was rising in a low spiral, perfect for a quick kick. He wriggled out of the crowd of bodies at the line of scrimmage and headed downfield, joining the pursuit of it.

The ball hit the ground near the twenty-yard line and took a high hop—a Sutton State bounce—continuing its way toward the Allerton goal. It bounded crazily along the ground, first going left, then going right.

An Allerton defensive halfback, running at full speed, approached the ball. Andy Sterling, one of the fastest Cowboys, was coming up behind him. The ball was on the twelve-yard line. It took another bounce. The Allerton defensive back bumped the ball. The ball bounced in front of him.

A shout went up from the Sutton State bench, and a giant roar rolled down onto the field from the 66,000 fans. Once touched by a defender, the ball was free. A fumble would belong to whichever team could gain possession.

The Allerton player, knowing he had no choice, grabbed for the ball. He scooped it in on the bounce. The roaring cheer faded as quickly as it had started. Then the Allerton player bobbled the ball, juggling it madly as he ran, trying to get a firm hold. At that moment, Andy slammed into him from the side. The ball squirted away, visible only a second before disappearing beneath a crowd of leaping, thrashing players —a mix of red jerseys with white numerals and white jerseys with green numerals.

Denny, too late to join in the scramble for the ball, stopped at the edge of the melee. The referee was digging through the pileup of players. He straightened.

He waved his arm in the direction of the Allerton goal. It was Sutton State's ball on the Allerton thirteen-yard line.

Denny shot a fist into the air. He heard the shouts from the Sutton State bench. Then he heard the roar of the crowd. The Sutton State players were swamping Boogie, who stood now with the ball in his hands, a wide grin on his face. Earthquake was slapping him on the back.

Denny ran over in front of the referee and made a T with his two hands, calling for a time out, and ran to the sideline.

Bucky Summers was waiting for him. For the first time in the four years that Denny had known the coach, Bucky Summers seemed excited. "Run Mark behind Earthquake, then Mike or Richie into the line," he said breathlessly. "Keep it in the line, straight into the line, nothing fancy. Plenty of time."

Denny nodded his head jerkily.

"Got it?" Summers asked.

"Yeah. Yeah."

Denny turned and jogged onto the field.

22

Denny leaned into the huddle and called two plays—Mark plunging over left tackle behind Earthquake, and Mike plunging between Earthquake and Dan Graham. Calling for a long count, he said, "Quick-start six." A five-yard penalty for an off-side violation would be mighty handy here.

"Hut-hut . . . hut . . . hut . . . hut . . . hut."

The Allerton linemen did not take the bait. They held their ground.

Denny took the snap. He pivoted and handed the ball off to Mark, who charged into the line. Mark, his legs pumping, followed Earthquake, then spun off to the side and went down. He gained two yards, to the Allerton eleven-yard line. Mike, on the quick snap without a huddle, got three yards, and Mark, with a tremendous second effort, gained three more.

The series of downs added up to a total gain of eight yards, to the Allerton five-yard line—two yards short of a first down and five yards short of a touchdown.

Denny called time out and jogged to the sideline where Polk and Summers were waiting.

"I'll run it in," Denny panted. "A roll-out, a quarterback keeper."

Polk stared down at Denny as if the quarterback had taken leave of his senses. Summers gaped at him blankly.

"They've been ignoring me all day," Denny said, rushing the words. "They act like I'm not even out there on the field. They don't even watch me. They won't be watching me this time." He was grinning now. "I can make 'em regret it."

Polk was silent. He gazed past Denny at the players gathered near the goal line. He glanced up at the scoreboard—probably checking the clock, Denny figured—and then he looked back at Denny.

"He's right," Summers said suddenly. "They have been ignoring him. They're convinced he's not going to do anything but hand off the ball. It might catch them flat-footed."

Denny was nodding his head in agreement with Summers. He knew that the smart play, the odds-on play, was *anything* but Denny Westbrook carrying the ball. Mark or Mike or Richie might make the two yards for a first down, if not the five for the touchdown. But Denny Westbrook?

"All right, son," Polk said quietly. "You run it in."

Denny nodded and ran back on the field. Leaning into the huddle, his first thought was, What have I done? But he wiped it from his mind and spoke to the team, choosing his words carefully.

"Quarterback roll-out right," he said slowly. He paused, letting the words sink in. The players around him in the huddle blinked. Then their eyes widened.

Mark Madison grinned. "I think it may work," he said.

"It'd better," somebody mumbled.

"Just make believe that I'm Louie," Denny said.

Denny broke the huddle, and the team lined up. He glanced at the goalposts in front of him. The crowd was strangely quiet. Or was it just that he could not hear them? Funny, he thought, how the two teams had battered each other for almost sixty minutes of playing time, and the outcome all came down to this one play. Win or lose? The question was going to be settled on this one play. In addition to the game, there were the national rankings, perhaps a national championship, surely a bowl bid all hinging on this one play.

He took a deep breath and barked the signals.

Dutch snapped the ball. Denny took the snap, pivoted, and extended the ball to Mark, crashing into the center of the line. At the last second, he withdrew the ball. He stepped back, the ball on his thigh, and then made an exaggerated motion of pitching out to Mike, racing to his left. The linebackers, sucked in by the fake to Mark, shifted their charge to follow

216

Mike. Denny replaced the ball on his thigh and turned. Then he tucked the ball away and began running parallel to the line of scrimmage.

Why couldn't he run faster? His feet felt as if they were carrying lead weights. Why couldn't he sail along with the easy strides of a Mike O'Brien? He felt as if his feet were tied together with a two-foot cord. He was in slow motion. The white jerseys of the Allerton defenders in front of him were in slow motion. The whole world was in slow motion.

Suddenly a white jersey loomed large in front of him. Denny veered. The white jersey went past him. He cut sharply to his left, heading straight for the goal line. There seemed to be an opening between the bodies. Something bumped him and then fell away. How long does it take to run five yards anyway?

Then there was nothing in front of him. He saw the wide stripe of the goal line. He dived for it. Again something bumped him, harder this time, and he hit the ground. He tried to turn over. Something was pinning his legs to the ground. He swiveled his head in time to see the referee throw his hand skyward—touchdown!

Denny got to his feet. He remembered all the fancy runners who liked to dance through the end zone, jubilantly waving the ball in the air while the crowd cheered. He remembered the cool ones, like Mike, who ignored the cheers, acting for all the world as if touchdowns were simply a routine thing. Denny handed the ball to the referee and turned to walk off the field.

From somewhere, far off in the distance, he heard the roar of the crowd pouring down from all sides. A television cameraman, with his portable camera on his shoulder, weaved into view in front of Denny. Instinctively Denny smiled into the camera. He kept walking.

Then he was swamped. As suddenly as if a dam had broken, a wave of bodies—all of them wearing red jerseys with white numerals—surrounded Denny. He was patted, pummeled, shoved, jabbed. He heard people calling his name. For a moment, his feet left the ground. He was being lifted. Then his feet regained the ground. The noise—the shouts, the laughter—closed in on him like a blanket.

The onslaught stopped as quickly as it had started. He was alone again. Somebody pounded him on the shoulder pad, but when he turned no one was there.

He pulled his chin strap loose, took off his helmet, and ran the rest of the way to the bench. Along the way, players held out their hands, palms up, and Denny slapped each of them.

At the bench, Bucky Summers threw an arm around Denny's shoulder and squeezed. Wally Polk was staring at the players on the field. Lamar Henry was kneeling for the snap. Sandy Ruzzo was readying himself for the kick.

218

Denny looked at the scoreboard. It read: Cowboys 15, Visitors 14.

Dutch snapped the ball. Lamar took it in. He placed it down. Sandy stepped forward. He kicked.

The scoreboard blinked: Cowboys 16, Visitors 14. The clock showed two minutes and forty-five seconds remaining.

Denny sat on a bench, slumped back against a locker, in the wake of the pandemonium of the winners' dressing room. The shouting and the cheering had died away. Most of the players, their uniforms removed, were making the trek to the showers. Denny sat unmoving, wearing a silly grin. He gulped in huge breaths of air. He puffed out his cheeks and exhaled.

They had done it. They had won. They had won with Denny Westbrook at quarterback.

To be sure, Denny knew that his quarterbacking was far—quite far—down the list of factors bringing the victory home to the Sutton State Cowboys. There was the defense, magnificent as they stopped the Allerton Lions time and again. There was the kicking of Sandy Ruzzo, which accounted for ten of the Cowboys' sixteen points. There was the work of the offensive line—Earthquake and Dan and Boogie and the rest of them—holding out the Allerton defenders so Denny could execute the plays. There were the runs of Mark and Richie and Mike. There was the receiving of Tim—a big play on the halfback pass, a miracle catch on Denny's throw over center. And then, down near the bottom of the list, was the quarterbacking of Denny Westbrook. That was the way Denny listed the reasons for the victory.

But nobody else listed them that way.

In the wild melee at the finish, Denny was the center of it all. The players mobbed him at the sideline when the gun sounded the end of the game. They tried to lift him and carry him off the field. Denny, alarmed, wriggled free. The jubilant players, with Denny in their midst, raced to the dressing room. Inside, they mobbed Denny again, everyone trying to get a hand on him—a jostle of the head, a clap on the shoulder pads, a slap on the hand. The noise was deafening. Denny's teammates were all around him—Boogie, Tim, Earthquake, even Mike and Dutch—and they all were laughing, shouting, cheering. They were calling his name.

"See, little fella," Earthquake said with a leer, "I told you we were going to make a hero out of you, didn't I?"

Denny returned the grin.

Somebody across the room shouted. "Hey, superstar, are you going to let Louie have his job back?"

Denny leaned toward the sound of the voice and said, "Louie who?"

Everybody roared.

Wally Polk approached. The crowd of players

parted. The shouting died down. The coach, his thin gray hair windblown, looked down at Denny for a moment without speaking. Then he grinned and shook his head slowly from side to side, as if still in utter disbelief. "Good game," he said.

"Thanks," Denny said.

Polk turned and walked away. The players began drifting toward their lockers. Denny called out, "Coach!" Polk stopped and turned. Denny walked up to him.

"What is it?" Polk asked.

The two were alone at the edge of the dressing room.

"Coach, I never forgot for a minute that the vote —"

Polk frowned. "The vote? What vote?"

Denny grinned at him. "The vote was six to one."

Wally Polk stared at Denny for a moment. Slowly his face broke into a wide smile. He extended a long arm around Denny's shoulder. Then he put the other arm around Denny and embraced him in a huge bear hug.

About the Author

Thomas J. Dygard was born in Little Rock, Arkansas, and received a B.A. degree from the University of Arkansas, Fayetteville. He began his career as a sportswriter for the *Arkansas Gazette* in Little Rock and joined the Associated Press in 1954. Since then, he has worked in A.P. offices in Little Rock, Detroit, Birmingham, New Orleans, and Indianapolis. At present, he is Chief of Bureau in Chicago.

Mr. Dygard is married, has two children, and now lives in Arlington Heights, Illinois.